THE PREACHER STORY

THE PREACHER STORY

Oladayo Sanusi

iUniverse, Inc.
New York Lincoln Shanghai

The Preacher Story

iUniverse books may be ordered through booksellers or by contacting:

iUniverse
2021 Pine Lake Road, Suite 100
Lincoln, NE 68512
www.iuniverse.com
1-800-Authors (1-800-288-4677)

Because of the dynamic nature of the Internet, any Web addresses or links contained in this book may have changed since publication and may no longer be valid.

This is a work of fiction. All of the characters, names, incidents, organizations, and dialogue in this novel are either the products of the author's imagination or are used fictitiously.

ISBN: 978-0-595-47387-8 (pbk)
ISBN: 978-0-595-91665-8 (ebk)

Printed in the United States of America

Introduction

A man walked up to me and asked me, "Do you have formal training in art?" I said no.

He asked me, "So why are you a painter?"

And I replied, "Because I love to paint."

He was about to walk away, but he paused and asked me another question. "So, how did you learn how to write?"

I looked him in his face and answered his question in a solemn voice. "Because I love to write," I said, slowly and methodically.

I thought he would walk away at that point, but he became more inquisitive, and he would not let go. He asked me another question.

"Now, you want to tell me you are a painter, a writer and a doctor? What time do you have to doctor your patients?"

I did not look away from his face and I responded, "My patients are not doctored. They simply need someone to take care of their medical problems. They need someone that will partner with them to take control of their lives, that will help them to be in charge of their disease process and to take control of their whole healing process."

At this point, I thought that he was satisfied. But he asked me another question. "So, what time do you have for your family?"

I responded, "I am a sojourner. I am a storyteller. I live for everybody. My family knows who I am. I am what I am—a smiling face that brings joy to a troubled soul."

I thought, now it is my turn to ask him a question, and I placed my hand on his shoulder.

"Would you like to listen to my story?"

CHAPTER 1

▼

It was a bright Thursday morning. The sky was a brilliant blue, with thin wisps of clouds dotting the horizon. Dr. Mars pulled his black sedan up to the back of his office and parked in the spot marked "Dr. Filip Mars." He looked at himself in the rearview mirror and paused to brush a crumb out of his short, brown mustache. He got out of the car and opened his back door, removing his freshly laundered, bright white lab coat.

He walked in through the back door and through the lounge area, straight down the hallway to his waiting room without stopping in his office. The small waiting room had a row of blue upholstered chairs against the far wall, facing the reception window. Stacks of newspapers and old magazines were spread across a low table in front of the chairs, with headlines proclaiming the latest exercise tips and ways to charm members of the opposite sex to the patients waiting to see the doctor. Four patients were already waiting, paging through the magazines and playing with their cell phones. Three students also sat in the waiting area, looking shyly at each other and the patients around them.

The three students stood as he came in. He strode up to him, walking with a slight swagger, his chest pushed out confidently. He shook each of their hands and introduced himself to them.

"My name is Dr. Filip Mars, and you must be the new medical students starting rotation in our small clinic."

The three students smiled, and he introduced himself to them one at a time. He thought that they looked very young, and he tried to picture himself in their shoes when he was a medical student in Europe more than two decades ago.

"What is your name?"

The first student introduced herself. Her hand seemed very small in his large palms, which had always been just slightly too big in proportion to his otherwise trim frame. "My name is Eva Holloway. I'm a third year medical student, and I just want to say thank you for the opportunity to do my rotation here."

Eva was a short, petite woman with a round, plump face and long, blonde hair. She looked even younger than the other students, and if not for her loud voice and firm handshake, she might have seemed out of place in the professional atmosphere.

Dr. Mars turned to the second student, a tall lady who was very slim, but had broad shoulders that were especially noticeable because she kept her dark brown hair short like a man's, clipped neatly around her ears. "My name is Melissa Yard, but you can call me Mel."

He turned back to Eva Holloway. "So, what can we call you?"

Eva blushed and responded hesitantly, "Just call me ... well, Eva." She laughed.

Dr. Mars turned back to Melissa and said, "What year are you?"

Melissa said she was also a third year medical student.

The third student was a young man who, like Melissa, had broad shoulders. His came with a stockier frame and a bright, almost comic smile. Yet, he looked very serious and academic, in part due to his glasses, with rims so thin that Dr. Mars could barely make them out.

He said to Dr. Mars, "My name is Donald Bunks. You can call me Don."

"Good," said Dr. Mars. "And what year are you?"

"I'm a fourth year student."

Dr. Mars led his new students from the waiting room through the door to the nurse's station, a small area behind a high counter where two women sat. Both looked up from their computers, where they had been reviewing the information for the patients the doctor was about to see.

"We are a very small clinic here, with only two nurses," Dr. Mars told his students. "We run Monday through Friday, 8 a.m. to 5 p.m. This is my staff."

Dr. Mars gestured to the first nurse, who stood as she spoke. Standing, the small woman was not much taller than she had been while seated.

"This is Cima Trotford. It's a difficult name, so sometimes I call her CT, just like a CAT scan. You'll have to ask her if you can call her that, too."

Cima said hello. "I'll let you call me CT if I like you," she said, squinting at the students. "I'm sure I will," she added, grinning.

The second nurse had turned to collect some papers, but she came back to the counter when Dr. Mars spoke her name. She looked stern but polite, with a high forehead and grayish-brown hair pulled back in a loose bun at the top of her head.

"This is Angelina Golden. I call her Angelou, or, if you like, Angel Gold," the doctor said affectionately.

Angelina smiled and placed her paper in front of her as she started typing.

Dr. Mars led the students back to the front of the office. They stood looking at the waiting room, but this time, it was from the inside of the receptionist's window.

Dr. Mars introduced the receptionist. "This is Martha Martin."

Martha greeted the students warmly, setting down the carton of orange juice she had been sipping. "You can call me M&M," she said, gesturing to a glass jar next to her computer that was filled with the colorful chocolate candies.

The students laughed, and Dr. Mars led them back down the clinic's hallway to his private office. It was larger than the nurse's station, with black wood furniture and a large, padded chair. Gifts from patients lined a bookcase behind the doctor's desk, with bobble head figurines and plaques bearing inspirational sayings mingling with medical dictionaries and reference books. The doctor's diploma hung on the wall next to a wedding photograph.

Dr. Mars led the patients back down the hallway to the five examination rooms. As they passed the receptionist's window, one of the patients, a very fat middle-aged woman, caught Don's eye. She smiled and winked, shaking her newspaper in his direction.

The doctor and students passed by and looked at each of the examination rooms, which each held a basic examination table, an otoscope for examining patients' eyes and ears, a blood pressure monitor, and a computer attached to the wall. Dr. Mars took the students into one of the examination rooms and demonstrated how the computer worked by flipping it open from the wall. All of the computers were programmed to accept voice commands, and Dr. Mars showed them how spoken words appeared in type on the screen.

"Technology these days," Mel mused softly.

They went to the lounge area at the back of the clinic, and he assigned them each a locker where they could keep their bags and valuables while they were doing rotation in his office. Besides his own locker and those of his staff, there were only two available spaces. Mel and Eva agreed to share a locker.

"Don't steal my purse," Mel said.

"Oh, I'd never," Eva said, not sure whether Mel was serious.

"Don't worry, Hon. There's nothing worth stealing in there anyway," Mel joked.

Dr. Mars asked the students if any of them had questions before they started seeing the patients. They all said no.

"Let's get started, then," Dr. Mars said. "First, let's have a talk about how I operate my clinic."

The doctor sat down at the long table in the break room. The students sat across from him. He told them that as a general practitioner, most of his patients came in with simple symptoms like headaches, earaches, and abdomen pain. He also told them that in the mornings, he did rounds at the hospital before he came in to the clinic. In the evening he said he went back to the hospital to do rounds again while finishing his notes for the clinic, all by dictation and voice commands on the hospital's similar computer system.

"Papers are crude. They're history. The way I operate is by using modern technology," Dr. Mars said. He went on about his procedures for seeing patients.

"The way I see patients is very detailed. I spend a very long time with new patients. I have them tell me their story. In fact, I'm a storyteller myself," he said.

"Really?" Don asked. "Are you a writer?"

Dr. Mars thought for a moment before he answered. "I do like to write," he replied. "Poetry, in fact."

He quickly changed the topic back to the patients. "When they finish telling me their story, it will reveal what is wrong with them, how to treat them, and how we will go about to manage their problems. Most of the time, when patients come in here, they have a long list of problems. I am not like some other doctors who tell them, 'We can only fix one thing a day.' All I do is listen and figure out what we need to fix." As he spoke, Dr. Mars stroked his black stethoscope. The instrument hung around his short, sturdy neck like a prizewinner's medallion.

"I fix that, and I fix it totally until the patient is happy and satisfied. By the time I fix the main problem, a lot of the laundry list may be taken care of, because many of the problems are usually symptoms of the main complaint."

Eva and Mel nodded. Don looked slightly bored, fidgeting in his seat.

"As we see patients together, you will understand the way I triage my patients and I relate to them. Sometimes I am very strict with these patients. The reason I am strict is that they tend to take so much time and act like babies. They become selfish, and they don't want to leave to make space for the next person."

Don perked up. He seemed more interested in the doctor's philosophy than the workings of the clinic.

Dr. Mars took the students back into his office and pulled the first patient's information up on the computer.

"As I mentioned, we're going to try to make it a little faster for patients that have follow ups, but we will spend more detailed time with new patients, always," Dr. Mars said.

His took the three students into the first examination room, where his first patient of the day was already waiting. She was a lady in her mid-forties, and when they came in, she was already lying down on the examination table.

"Hi, Paula," Dr. Mars said congenially. "Why are you in such a hurry to be lying down instead of sitting up?"

Paula grimaced and responded, "I have severe abdominal pain."

"That is not good. We don't like that," Dr. Mars said. He moved closer to her, put gloves on his large hands, and checked her blood pressure.

"No, Doc, you don't need to check my blood pressure," Paula yelped. "My blood pressure is always fine. The abdomen is where I'm having a lot of problems. I've also been having a lot of nausea, and I've been vomiting."

He put his stethoscope on her belly and checked it. He turned to the students, who were hovering nervously by the door. "Look, I don't think she's tender," He told them. He had each of them put their own stethoscopes on the patient's stomach. He noticed that Eva's stethoscope was pink.

Dr. Mars smiled and said to the students, "You know, here in the U.S., we do tests to diagnose everything. Where I trained in Europe, we didn't do that. We felt, we listened, and we touched. The first time I heard a doctor say that we were going to do a CAT scan of the abdomen to diagnose appendicitis, I said to myself, 'This must be a joke.' I thought it was a major waste of resources. How do you diagnose appendicitis with a CAT scan? It's either there or it's not there, and if it's there and you think it's the cause of the pain, go in and take it out."

He looked again at Paula and he asked his students, "What do you think is going on with this lady?"

Mel was the first to answer. She said, "I think this is abdominal pain associated with nausea and vomiting."

Dr. Mars said, "Yes, clearly."

Then Donald cut in. "It may be diverticulitis."

Dr. Mars said, "Diverticulitis? How old are you?" he asked the patient.

"I'm 39," Paula responded, looking anxiously at Don.

"You want to change your answer?" Dr. Mars asked Don. Don said nothing.

Eva cut in. "If I would make one guess, I would think this is appendicitis."

"Why do you think this is appendicitis?" Dr. Mars asked.

Eva said, "Can I ask the patient one question?"

"Go ahead, be my guest."

"Have you been having any fever?" Eva asked. The patient answered no.

"Have you been having diarrhea?" she followed.

"No," Paula said, looking worried.

"I need to send you to the hospital," Dr. Mars said. "This is the United States, and we have to do the proper thing the way they want us to do it. We are going to have you have a CT scan to prove that this is appendicitis, and I will have you admitted to the hospital and have the surgeon take it out. When in doubt, just take it out," he chimed, touching the patient's hand affectionately. He called for his nurse to come and prepare the patient for admission to the hospital.

Eva asked Mel, "So, I'm right?" Mel turned to Don, who rolled his eyes.

Dr. Mars smiled at Eva. "I think so, but you didn't tell me why you are right. You want to guess?"

Eva started to speak, but faltered. "No, you tell me," she said.

He said, "First and foremost, the pain is localized to the right iliac fossa. The pain is not tender, but she has rebound tenderness and a guarding sign. She is in her forties, so she is still at the age where she could develop appendicitis."

"Isn't appendicitis more common in children and the elderly?" Don asked, pushing his glasses up on the bridge of his nose.

"Yes, that's true, appendicitis is more common at the two extremes of life. But there is no rule that it can't occur at any point in time. From the clinical description she is giving me and my physical examination, it is appendicitis. You want to bet?" Dr. Mars challenged.

They all shook their heads no.

As they were preparing to go into the next exam room, Dr. Mars told the students, "You have to be out of the loop. There is a loop that tricks you into the system. The system trains you not to believe your fingers and your stethoscope. It trains you only to believe in tests, and not to believe in your own hands. The system tells you not to believe in listening to the patients, because patients are just liars. It tells you not to trust the patients, because the patients are just here to make money out of your mistakes."

"But haven't you ever been sued for medical malpractice?" Mel asked.

"I have. We all have," Dr. Mars replied. "But the problem is that fear of getting sued forces you into the loop, where all you and I are trained to do is to work with the system. If the patient coughs, we order a chest X-ray. If the patient sneezes, we order allergy tests. If the patient has diarrhea, we order a stool workup. If the patient has abdominal pain, we don't even touch them before we order the CAT scan."

Dr. Mars paused. "I'll tell you what—I've never lost a malpractice suit. But still, it's difficult to stay out of that loop, because if you end up getting sued and you lose, you get burned. Your very own attorneys, your very own teachers will ask you, 'Why didn't you order the MRI, why didn't you order the CT scan, why didn't you order all these tests? Maybe you would have found something.'"

Dr. Mars tapped his forehead. "Perhaps we need to scan the patients here in order to look for lies," he said.

The students laughed. When it was quiet, he told them seriously, "Look, that loop is called the system. And we are the ones that are making the system work."

"I don't know if I understand," Eva said. "Can you give us an example of a time when tests are really unnecessary?"

"Of course," Dr. Mars said. "The other night, I was in the hospital, and I went to place a nasogastric tube in a patient whose abdomen was very distended. After I placed the NG tube, I listened and heard the tube was in place, and everything was fine as far as I was concerned. Does that sound reasonable to you?"

"Sure," Eva responded.

"Well, I certainly agree. However, I did not know the protocol of this particular hospital, and while I was leaving, the nurse asked me where they could call me to take a look at the X-ray. I asked her, 'X-ray of what?' She said, 'We have to take an X-ray of the abdomen to make sure that the NG tube is properly placed.'"

He frowned at the students. "You pass the NG tube through and you listen with your stethoscope. You put bubbles of air in it, and you can be sure it's there just by listening. You don't need to do an X-ray for that, do you?"

"Maybe not," Don said, thinking. Eva nodded.

"So, I told the charge nurse, 'If it's part of your protocol, do the X-ray. If the radiologist on call can take a look at it for me, that would be fine.' I signed my name on the paper and I left. And I thought, I am part of this loop, this system. I have become a robot that cannot diagnose pneumonia by listening with my stethoscope. I have to diagnose only through a chest X-ray."

The three students looked surprised. Don asked him, "So by listening to a patient, you can know that it is just pneumonia?"

"Yes, why not?" Dr. Mars said. "What are the symptoms of pneumonia? Shortness of breath, the patient has a fever, he is dyspneic. You listen, you hear bronchial breath sound, you hear crackles, and you can feel the enlarged nodes. You don't have to work the patient up and down with investigations."

Don asked him again, "But how do you differentiate between pneumonia, congestive heart failure, and a pleural effusion?"

Dr. Mars said, "Does the patient with congestive heart failure come to you with fever?"

"No," Don said.

"When you tap on the patient's chest, if there is plural effusion, wouldn't there be dullness?"

Don said, "That's true."

Dr. Mars said, "We have to stop being robots. We have to be able to make clinical decisions and diagnoses based on our findings, and proceed to treating the patients appropriately. I agree with everybody that this process, at times, becomes very confusing. A patient with congestive heart failure may have super-imposed pneumonia and superimposed effusion. All three can happen to one person. But the Good Lord has given us the knowledge to decipher and go ahead and treat these patients. If based on clinical suspicion, we have reason to believe that a patient has all three together, treat all the three."

Dr. Mars put his hand on the knob of the second patient's examination room. "Why wait for the investigation reports?" he asked. "Don't send them to X-ray or CT scan without starting treatment. Don't be part of the loop of the system when you are triaging a patient that is very sick and has three things wrong at the same time."

His next patient was new to the practice. She was a middle-aged lady who was quite obese, weighing about 260 pounds. She had very chubby cheeks. Don recognized her as the woman who had winked at him from the waiting room.

"How old are you?" Dr. Mars asked.

She said, "I am 46 years old and I'm a diabetic."

Dr. Mars said, "Let's not get ahead of ourselves! How do you know you are diabetic?"

She glanced at the medical students, smiled, and responded, "I went to a health fair. At that fair, they checked our blood sugar, and they noticed that mine was high. They asked me to get in touch with a local doctor. Your name was given to me, and I was told you were very good and could help me with my diabetes."

The patient went on. "Every member of my family is diabetic. My father, my mother, my aunts—everybody. They're all diabetic. So I'm not surprised that I am, too."

She turned to Don. "Do you have diabetes in your family, Hon?"

Before Don could reply, Dr. Mars asked quickly, "What other problems does your family have?"

"Apart from sugar, they have high blood pressure. Thank God I don't have that," she said. She winked at Don, who scooted a few feet back, behind Mel. Mel gave him a wink, too.

"How do you know that?" Dr. Mars asked, sounding dejected.

"Oh, they checked that at the health fair, too. They told me it wasn't high; in fact, they said it was very good."

"Okay, what else do they have?" Dr. Mars asked.

"They have high cholesterol, but not me."

"And how do you know *that*?"

"Health fair," she retorted. Eva looked at Mel and Don, and all three looked at the doctor to see his reaction. He appeared tired.

"Okay, any other history of family problems?"

"Yes, cancer. A lot of cancer in the family," the patient said glumly.

"What type of cancer?" Dr. Mars asked.

"Breast, colon, brain, head, neck. Name it, they've all got it."

Dr. Mars finally laughed. "Wow, what kind of family are you from?" he said jokingly.

The patient responded seriously. "Unhappily, a family of very sick people. All of them are very, very sick."

Dr. Mars asked her a final question. "Is there anybody in your family that sees a psychiatrist?"

The patient frowned at him, looking angry. "No, nobody in my family sees a psychiatrist. Nobody in the family is crazy—they're sick! They have high blood sugar, the high blood pressure, cholesterol, heart problems, and cancer, but they are *not* crazy."

Dr. Mars had the students take the rest of the history on the patient and led them through a basic examination. He shook the patient's hand and called Cima in, asking the nurse to arrange for the tests to be done and to schedule a follow-up appointment for the patient when the results arrived in two weeks.

The patient asked, "Dr. Mars, are you going to give me any medications?"

He said "Not yet. Not until I get the test results back in two weeks. Then, we'll have your reports waiting for you, and we'll talk about starting medications if and when the time is right."

After the patient left, Don asked if he could try dictating her history into the computer system.

"A lot of people go through labeled with so many strange conditions," Dr. Mars told Eva and Mel as Don played with the computer. "You know the one that really fascinates me?"

"What?" Mel asked.

"Chronic fatigue syndrome. As far as I am concerned, it's bullshit. They can't prove it exists, and if it does, does it really need treatment? I could say I'm chronically fatigued, but I have to go to work. I have to see my patients and get my paychecks. I may be tired, but I've got work to do. Try telling your professors at school that you failed your test because you couldn't study because of your chronic fatigue syndrome."

Mel chuckled. Eva looked at Don, who was trying to figure out how to delete the wrong word from the computer's screen. Discouraged, he asked what the doctor was talking about.

"Chronic fatigue syndrome, Don. It amazes me. I've seen a few patients come into my clinic and tell me, 'I have a diagnosis of chronic fatigue syndrome, and my doctors are treating me.' A lot of the time, the doctors are giving them antidepressants—they're giving them medications that are causing them all the time to be so sleepy and fatigued."

The students laughed. They saw several other patients with Dr. Mars before lunchtime. As they were about to take their break, Mel pulled a women's magazine from her locker.

"This yours?" she asked Eva.

"Nope," Eva said. "Must have been left there by the last med student."

Dr. Mars glanced at the magazine. He sighed. "Look at that actress, whoever she is. The human race has been insulted by practically every available means to look artificial. There are so many boobs; you don't even know what breasts are real anymore. The noses are all reshaped, and the jaws are lifted. Flaps are taken away by liposuction. These patients go on the Internet and sell themselves to the first doctor who offers a ten percent discount on cosmetic surgery."

"I would never get plastic surgery," Eva said resolutely. "Especially not from some hack off the Internet."

"The Internet certainly has its benefits," Dr. Mars said. "It's one of the wonders of our time, like the eighth wonder of the world. The computer has absolutely revolutionized the way we live, the way we do things, and the order of the day. But can you imagine what some people are using the Internet for? It's like a sex machine for them, using it to meet with kids in order to have sex with them."

Mel shook her head. "That's terrible," she said.

"The same thing goes for medicine," Dr. Mars said. "There's so much abuse."

Don cut in. He had been paging through the magazine from the locker, looking at the models. "It's not just cosmetic surgery, though. Right, Dr. Mars? People have all kinds of elective surgeries more often these days."

"Absolutely," Dr. Mars said, picking up the magazine from the break room table and tossing it in the trash. "People are being rushed too quickly into coronary artery bypass grafting, too. They just go in and replace valves and arteries too early. They cut and cut and cut. Pacemakers are now like fashion—everybody has one. You have to have one or the other, a pacemaker or an AICD. Even before they check your potassium and magnesium, before you can say, 'check,' the pacemaker is in place. Isn't that something?"

The students listened to him quietly as he finished. He told them he had to go to the hospital, and he would meet them in the afternoon. He gave them a one-hour break.

As Dr. Mars looked through his computer before he left, he realized that he had only seen four patients because he was so busy talking with the students, telling them stories and wiling away time.

Imagine you were him, with his big, protuberant belly and stinking groin. Is it lack of good shower? It is smelly, stinks, his groin, but they are screaming to get oxygen.

You paged the doctor. He called back in a jiffy, and told you to give oxygen. Of course you know that. Just because you are not the doctor does not mean you don't know you have to give oxygen.

You imagine you were in his shoes. Now you stuck a finger into your own very groin and at last, it stinks, coming from one job to the other.

Have you ever thought of listening to the grass?

After the break, the rest of the day went by very quickly. At one point, Dr. Mars' receptionist was passing through the corridor, and he called to her.

He said, "Martha Martin, M&M!"

She smiled and said, "Dr. Preacher, what have you got to say about me?"

The students laughed.

"We didn't know he was a preacher," Mel said.

"Though we may have had a suspicion," Don added.

M&M said to them, "Oh, we spend so much time waiting for him to finish with each patient because he's so busy preaching. Sometimes, the patients get so carried away with his talks that we're all here after dark."

CHAPTER 2

▼

Dr. Mars arrived in the clinic and his medical students were already waiting for him in the break room, chattering away.

"So, Mel, where are you from?" Dr. Mars asked.

"I was born in South Dakota, but I was raised in New York City," she answered.

"Both of them are very cold," Dr. Mars said.

"You're telling me! After being in New York City for years, I moved with my family to here in Texas."

"How do you like it here?" Dr. Mars asked.

"It's okay. It's a little bit hot, but it's okay," she said.

"So what do you plan to specialize in when you finish med school?"

Mel ran her fingers through her short hair. Today, her choppy bangs were pinned back with a gold barrette. "I plan to be an ophthalmologist," she said. "Ophthalmology has always been my passion, because I like to take care of delicate things like the eye."

"Maybe you can help me out, then," Don said, tapping the rim of his glasses.

Mel laughed. "Plus, I don't want to be on call all the time, and a lot of the eye emergencies can be managed whenever you can get there. Especially since I plan to have a family and raise my own children."

"Children?" Dr. Mars asked. "How many do you plan to have?"

"Five or six," Mel replied. Don laughed, and Mel shot him a glance. "Do you have any children?" Mel asked the doctor.

"No," he replied. "My wife, Lucinda, and I never wanted to have children. We're both so busy. She's in real estate. We decided to contribute to our community in other ways. Plus, you're going to have a hell of a time paying all those kids' ways through school!"

The doctor turned to Donald and said, "So, where are you from?"

Don replied, "I was born and raised in Texas."

"So you're a true cowboy, then. And how do you like my clinic?"

"I've learned a lot. I've done a couple of rotations with some other doctors in cardiology and GI," Don said.

"That's nice. And what would you like to do your residency training in?"

"I'd like to be an internist. I love internal medicine and general practice. I want to go into private practice."

Dr. Mars laughed and said, "Private practice is good, but it's tedious. You're on call, for the most part, all day. You have to control yourself in a private practice—you have no free time, and you aren't guaranteed money. It depends on how hard you work. Generally in life, I believe you cannot have time and money unless you are born with a silver spoon or you are doing something crooked. If you have time, you cannot have money, because to make money you need to work hard. If you want to work so hard, you cannot have time."

Mel turned to Don and asked playfully, "So, where's your spoon?"

Before he could respond, the doctor continued. "If you have the silver spoon, it's a different ballgame, because a lot of the time you have an inheritance waiting for you, so you can work less time and spend more money. Or you can do crooked things like cook the books, not see patients and write that you did, or spend five or ten minutes with each patient and give them the choice of fixing one problem per day."

"So, which one is it for you, Mel?" Don retorted back. "You look like a good cook …"

"Hush," Mel said. "After all, we can all see that Eva's the truly shady one."

Eva just blushed. The doctor smiled at her. "And what about you, Miss Eva Holloway? Where are you from?"

"I was also born and raised in Texas."

"And what do you plan to do your residency training in?"

"Well, for now, I haven't decided. But I'm really looking at going into surgery or gynecology."

"Either way, you'll be very busy," Dr. Mars responded. "Well, let's get down to business for the day and start to see patients."

Before they could leave the lounge area, one of his nurses, Angelina Golden, came in. "There's a man in the waiting area to see you, doctor. He said his name is Ben." She faltered when she said the word, 'man,' and she hesitated for a moment before adding, "I think he was a man, Dr. Mars. But I believe he may be a cross dresser—he's kind of dressed like a woman."

The doctor looked startled. "Ben? All right. He's my friend, my neighbor. He called me last night and said he wasn't feeling too well. I think you should put him in the system. Register him and I will see him."

As they headed down the hallway, Don asked him, "So what happened to Paula, the lady that we admitted to the hospital yesterday?"

Dr. Mars said, "Oh, I almost forgot. I was going to tell you about her. Of course, as I was mentioning yesterday, it's all about the loop, about what people expect us to do when diagnosing people. She, of course, had appendicitis. But she was very unfortunate. Her appendix had ruptured, and she was rushed to the operating room last night to have it taken out."

Eva looked worried and said, "But she didn't have any pain. She didn't have a fever. Why did she rupture, but there was no pain?"

"Any time there's a perforation or rupture in the abdomen, the omentum, which is a fat layer in the abdomen, actually condenses and walls off the inflammation," Dr. Mars said. "That's why we call the omentum 'the policeman of the abdomen.' It is one of the ways the Good Lord saves his own people from obvious disaster."

"I never knew that," Don said.

"You see, the other thing I keep telling everybody is that as a doctor, you should see yourself as a partner in the health and disease management process of your patients," Dr. Mars went on, standing near the nurses' station. "At times, you need to let them know that they have to stop their worrying. Like my friend who is sitting out there—he is worried that his blood sugar is too high because someone told him that his levels are inconsistent, and he has a lot of frequency going to the bathroom. He doesn't even have any evidence there is anything wrong with him. Patients like Paula, with appendicitis, have something to worry about. My friend probably doesn't, but I will take a look anyway."

Dr. Mars shook his head. "That's the way it goes. Some people just like to take the sick role. Some of my patients have been admitted to the hospital so many times that I can recite their histories off the top of my head like the national anthem. Nothing else is wrong with them. It's just that they have assumed the role of a sick patient, and any time anything goes wrong, they flee right into my examination room."

Don interrupted the doctor's thoughts. "Dr. Mars, I understand that hypochondriac patients might be annoying. But isn't it a doctor's job to listen to a patient's complaints, no matter what?"

Dr. Mars nodded at Don. "Yes, it is, and some patients may simply be unlucky and constantly sick. But that is usually not the case. Most of these repeat patients are not ready to partner with us in their own health care. They just want to be cared for constantly. They go to so many doctors, I call it doctor shopping. Each doctor does something, and no matter how many times the new doctors review their current medications, they keep hiding them."

"Isn't that dangerous?" Eva asked.

"Absolutely," Dr. Mars said. "You find out, for example, that a patient is on three different types of beta-blockers. They're on Metoprolol, Toprol, *and* Lopressor. And they come to you and their pulse rate is low and they pass out, and they go to the ER. You clean them up and they get beta-blocker withdrawal, because they aren't taking their meds anymore. Now they come back the next week with tachycardia and a pulse rate of 150. It's a vicious cycle."

The doctor looked exasperated, discouraged by patients' lack of control over their lives.

"It sounds like these patients just abuse the system, and there's not much we can do about it," Mel reflected.

"It's true that some of them can't be changed," Dr. Mars responded. "But you have to try. You need to talk to them and let them know that if anybody wants to give them a new medication, they need to ask you first, as their primary doctor, to review whether they need that medication and if there will be any interactions."

"But isn't that their new doctor's job?" Don asked. "Shouldn't they do a more thorough job of getting their patients' histories?"

Dr. Mars shook his head vigorously. "No, I don't think so. We, the doctors, are doing the best we can, but these patients go to so many hospitals and clinics that even they don't know what medications they're already on. What is the doctor supposed to do? He's not a mind reader; he's not a forecaster. So he gives them what he can, not knowing what they were already taking before. They go home and go back to what they were taking before plus the new one, and they get into trouble."

Angelina Golden came down the corridor looking for the doctor.

"Dr. Mars, the gentleman outside did not want to register. He said he's your friend and you promised to see him, and he doesn't want to pay us anything. He doesn't even want to sign a paper making a payment plan." Angelina wrung her hands together. Eva noticed that they were very delicate and small, nothing like the doctor's.

Dr. Mars said, "Well, he *is* my friend, my neighbor. He has some issues, a bit of a financial situation. Don't register him. Just get me his vital signs, put him in my office, and I'll come see him. Just let me know when he's ready to be seen, Angel Gold," he said sweetly, placing emphasis on her nickname.

The students finally accompanied the doctor into the room of the first patient that was waiting, noting that she was pacing the room. Dr. Mars went to her and introduced the students, and they started a conversation about why the patient was there. After seeing a few more patients, Angel Gold came back and told him that his friend, Ben, was ready to be seen and was in his office.

Dr. Mars excused himself from his students. He looked uncomfortable and ruffled, and sweat had broken on his wide forehead. "I want to see my friend personally, so he isn't worried," Dr. Mars explained, entering his personal office and closing the door quickly behind him.

In his office, Ben sat in the doctor's large, comfortable chair behind his desk, instead of in the smaller one meant for the patients. His tall, slim frame provided a stark contrast to his large, obviously fake breasts. Dr. Mars did not know how long Ben had had the implants, or for that matter, why he had ever gotten them. Ben was also wearing a low cut red shirt, and he had shaved his chest hair so that he appeared smooth like a woman's. His long, curly hair hung down on his chest, and he was wearing red hoop earrings in both ears and bright red lipstick that looked terrible matched with his pale skin. He grinned when Dr. Mars came in.

"Hello, Filip. I wanted to come see you."

Dr. Mars sighed. "Come on, Ben. You know you can't come see me here. I'll meet you later." He motioned for Ben to get up.

"But Filip, I told you I wasn't feeling good. I texted you last night, and you said you would check me out." He made an exaggerated pout with his ruby red lips.

"I didn't mean here, Ben. I meant in private."

In a few minutes, Dr. Mars came out of the room looking very irritated. He handed the chart that Angelina had made for Ben to the receptionist, M&M. As Ben headed for the door, Dr. Mars started toward the nurse's station, where his students were clustered, waiting for him.

M&M called to Dr. Mars as he walked away. "You didn't write anything on your friend's chart."

"Don't worry about it," Dr. Mars said dismissively. "There's nothing wrong with him. I just reassured him that he needs to take control of himself. I don't even think he has diabetes."

M&M said quietly, "We're not even sure—is 'he' a he or a she?"

Dr. Mars responded, "He likes to believe that he's a woman. He's been like that for some time. If he comes in again, please let me know before you put him in a room."

Going back to the students, the doctor realized that they seemed uncomfortable and worried. He told them to take an early break. He wiped sweat from his forehead, and the students thought that he looked harassed, like something had happened between him and the strange man that came in.

"Is everything okay?" Eva asked. "It looks like that man really upset you."

Dr. Mars said, "Yes, in a way he did. I've known him for a long time, and he's obviously very troubled. I've listened to him and assured him there's nothing wrong with him, but he wants to play the sick role. It's very disturbing."

The students excused themselves, and Dr. Mars continued to see patients. As he was about to go for his lunch break, M&M came and told him that the emergency room doctor was on the phone for him. He picked the phone up at the nurse's station and had a quick conversation with the ER doctor. When he finished, he looked even more frustrated and harried.

"I have to go to the ER. God, this is unbelievable," Dr. Mars told M&M. "I didn't know he was on methadone. He never told us about that."

M&M said, "Who is on methadone? Who would that be?"

"Mr. Tom Joseph," Dr. Mars replied. "I'll be back."

He walked out the back door to his sedan. As he drove to the emergency room, he realized he was clutching the steering wheel so hard that his knuckles were sore and tight.

When he arrived at the emergency room, he went to talk to the ER doctor first. "I can't believe Mr. Joseph is on methadone. He never told us," Dr. Mars told him. "The man is 66 years old, and I've been seeing him for nine months now. He never mentioned that he was a drug addict or that he was using methadone to recover. Let me go talk with him."

Dr. Mars went briefly behind one of the curtained areas where Mr. Joseph was waiting. He came out and told the ER doctor that they would need to admit him. "His volume is depleted, he's been throwing up, he has a lot of nausea, and he's very orthostatic. I couldn't even feel his pressure when he's sitting up. We'll need to contact his program and find out his dosage, and then give him some IV hydration and methadone."

The ER doctor shook his head. "I don't know how he got himself into this mess at 66," he said.

Dr. Mars agreed. "Being on methadone isn't good," he muttered, writing admitting orders on the patient before he left the emergency room and retunred to his office.

During the afternoon session, Dr. Mars was more jovial and composed. He told his students about Mr. Joseph, who had lost his methadone card and didn't get his weekend stock of the drug. He explained that, when he went back to the program on Monday, they didn't give him his methadone because he couldn't find his card. Being off the drug for several days had caused terrible withdrawal, with lots of diarrhea, nausea and vomiting.

Don was very interested in the methadone program, and he asked how it worked.

"On the weekends, most methadone programs aren't open, so they give the patients their supply to take on Saturday and Sunday. Lots of the patients are very happy because they can take a double dose or sell it on the street. Isn't that nice? That's where our tax money goes."

With a snort, Dr. Mars led the students into the exam room to see the next patient. She was 90 years old and had been brought into the clinic by her grandson, who wasn't in the room with her.

Dr. Mars knew the patient, and he knew she didn't have very good cognitive function and was supposed to be accompanied by someone in the clinic. "Who came with you? Why are you by yourself?" he asked her.

The patient looked at Dr. Mars and said, "Who are you?"

"Come on, you forgot me already?" Dr. Mars laughed. He explained to the students that the patient was often disoriented.

"No, I'm not!" the patient said angrily. "I just don't like it when you come smiling into my face like that!"

Dr. Mars put his hand forward and said, "I'm not smiling in your face, dear. I'm just here to shake your hand and say, 'Happy dementia!'"

The lady looked confused for a moment. Then she smiled, shook his hand, and said to him, "Happy dementia to you as well!"

The med students laughed. They proceeded to review her medications, and Dr. Mars told them another story.

"I like how this patient wished me happy dementia," he said. "It made me recall when I was a first year resident. We had a patient come in with a blood creatinine of 18. I spoke to the patient and he was stable, not having any signs of arrhythmia. His blood pressure was very high, but he was awake and alert, and his blood urine reagent was like 90. What would you do at that point, Don?"

Don didn't hesitate to answer. "I would order dialysis for the patient," he said proudly.

"Very good, Don. So after I presented the patient to my chief resident, he asked me to start collecting 24-hour urine because he wanted to know the creatinine clearance for this patient. I said, 'What if it is 30 percent? What if it is 50 percent? He needs dialysis no matter what. Why do I have to do creatinine clearance?'"

"Too many tests," Eva said, repeating the doctor's favorite mantra.

"Too many tests," he agreed. "I wish I had told my chief resident, 'Happy dementia!'"

The 90-year-old patient asked him, "Did you do that?"

Dr. Mars laughed. "No, I could not. It was my chief resident. If I did, I would be in big trouble."

The next patient was an obese man in his forties who weighed 260 pounds. He was full of complaints, and he told Dr. Mars, "I don't know why they won't approve me for disability."

"Your insurance? Why would they approve you for disability?" Dr. Mars asked.

"I cannot walk," the patient complained. "I've been trying to get a job forever, and it took them almost three years to approve me for Medicaid. I'm not getting any checks, I can't work, and my back is very bad. I've had two surgeries already on this back, and I cannot walk."

Dr. Mars said, "We'll see what we can do to help you. You should probably get a disability lawyer, and my nurses can arrange for your records here to be sent to him."

"Can you give me a letter saying that I'm disabled?" the patient asked.

The doctor looked up from his watch, which he had been using to mark time while taking the patient's pulse. "Mr. Watts, is it just your back that's giving you problems? Are you walking with a cane?"

"No," the patient said, almost defiantly.

"Are you using a walker?"

"No."

"You are not in a wheelchair."

"No, hell no! Who wants to be in a wheelchair?"

"I can't say you're disabled, then," the doctor said softly. "Get a lawyer and sort this out with them, and if they need us to fill out papers regarding your medical condition, have them send it to us."

After leaving the exam room, Mel was flustered. "Why does that man think he's disabled? If he loses weight, his back will probably be better and he'll be able to walk just fine."

Dr. Mars said, "Now you're thinking like a true, disillusioned doctor, Mel. Let's ask our next patient what he thinks about Mr. Watts' condition."

They went into the next room, where a 66-year-old gentleman who had undergone coronary artery bypass grafting was waiting. His chart stated that he had chronic obstructive pulmonary disease and diabetes. He was also on oxygen, and his tank sat by the side of his wheelchair, which he used because a stroke had left him paralyzed on one side.

Dr. Mars shook his hand. "Mr. Stevens, it's been a long time! How have you been doing? You missed two of your appointments, what's been going on?"

"Doc, with you, it's always a pleasure," Mr. Stevens responded. "I've just been so busy at the office, I've been leaving at 9 p.m. every day. This is our busy season, and we're getting a lot of supplies and things to do. It's not like I don't want to come in and do my checkup, but I have to take care of these things."

Dr. Mars asked Mr. Stevens how he was feeling.

"I have issues—sometimes I feel more like I'm 90 years old. But I'm hanging in there and trying to do my best," he said.

Dr. Mars turned to his students. "The gentleman you just saw was 42 and wouldn't do anything because of a bad back. Yet here is Mr. Stevens, who is 66, in a wheelchair, has had COPD, and still runs his own business."

"If I don't do it, nobody will," Mr. Stevens said.

Dr. Mars said, "This is what we call abuse of the system. A lot of people who do not need disability get all sorts of benefits from the government, while those who truly need it are not getting anything."

After saying goodbye to Mr. Stevens, Dr. Mars explained insurance fraud. "We slave in vain for these people who are frequent fliers of the hospital. They know how to abuse the system, and when they get inside the hospital, you can't get them out. They see the hospital system as a hotel—when they check out of one, they check into another. They want their breakfast in bed and the nurses to wipe their butts. They have walkers, scooters, and motorized wheelchairs. They don't even need these things. They just want to keep them to get disability status."

"It sounds like a big mess. Is there something we can do about it?" Eva asked.

Dr. Mars said, "It's not a single-person task. We have to let the patients know that a lot of things that we're doing to them are not needed. For example, I've seen a lot of 90 year olds on dialysis. Why should someone who has lived for so many years want to depend on a machine to crank up his system three times a week? Then when he doesn't get it, he gets so sick because of the excessive wear and tear on his body. As doctors, we should be more realistic with our patients and explain that constant medication and treatment is not always the best option."

"You're right," Mel said. "I had an aunt who died of brain cancer. There was no way she was going to survive, but they kept doing surgery and chemotherapy, just because she couldn't let go." Mel gave a small smile, shrugging her shoulders.

"Exactly," Dr. Banks said. "Why should we continue to give chemotherapy when they have terminal cancer? I've seen an 85-year-old lady with a terminal malignancy in her colon on dialysis. I asked myself, what is this dialysis for? And the patient herself does not really even know what the doctors are doing to her system."

Dr. Banks dropped a few charts off at the nurse's station. "And the government is not checking this—there are no balances. A lot of patients have been diagnosed by psychiatrists as being bipolar. I told one patient who was always in the emergency room, "You may be bipolar—or it could be all the cocaine you take. As far as I'm concerned, if he's bipolar, I'm tripolar."

Mel laughed. "You're tripolar?"

"Oh yes, I'm tripolar," Dr. Mars said, twirling his finger near his temple. "But with my tripolarity, I manage to be here, working for my paycheck and seeing patients. Unlike most patients who believe they are bipolar, I have a grip on my life. And unlike most alcoholics, I know how to drink without getting drunk, and if I did, I would know how to put myself to bed and sleep it off instead of coming into the ER to abuse the system."

Don looked slightly frustrated with the doctor's lecture. "It seems like you don't believe in so many things that they've taught us in med school are essential. What about antibiotics? If we don't' give antibiotics and there's an infection, the patient could die."

Dr. Mars looked at him and said, "Antibiotics, discovered by Alexander Fleming. He discovered penicillin could be used for a good cause. But look at what's going on today—we have so many antibiotics that we've created super bugs. When God gives us knowledge and the ability to intervene in the disease process, we overdo it. We prescribe antibiotics for every patient, even if they sneeze."

"But some patients need antibiotics," Mel stated in a questioning tone.

"We can use regular, small doses of antibiotics," Dr. Mars said. "Patients with a sore throat need, at the most, penicillin. But they'd rather go to doctors that will prescribe them stronger antibiotics, and then they grow super bugs and are constantly sick."

After attending patients for the rest of the day, Dr. Mars dismissed the students. As they left the clinic, his beeper sounded.

Dr. Mars called the emergency room and spoke to the physician who had paged him. The doctor told him that he had a patient who needed dialysis, but the patient couldn't be seen by a nephrologist until Dr. Mars admitted him.

Dr. Mars drove quickly to the emergency room. At the ER, he went to see the patient, a middle-aged man who was very short of breath and couldn't even speak a complete sentence. The doctor examined him briefly and told him that he needed to get dialysis and that he would call the nephrologist.

The patient gasped for air as he said, "No, I don't want dialysis."

"If you don't want dialysis, you shouldn't have come to the emergency room," Dr. Mars said sternly. "If you knew you didn't want dialysis, you should have stayed home and not wasted everybody's time. I'm going to ask for a surgery to have a catheter put in your neck for the dialysis."

He continued to examine the patient, and he noticed that the patient had a shunt on his left arm. "What is all this talk about not getting dialysis?" he asked the patient. "You already have a shunt, haven't you been on it before?"

The patient said, "Hell no! My doctor put it there to give me dialysis, but I refused."

Dr. Mars turned his back to the patient and tensed one fist, fixating on the wall. Then, he turned back and explained the situation to the patient calmly and slowly. "You let them put a shunt in your arm, but you don't want dialysis? It looks like you're wasting my time here. I'm going to go speak to the nephrologist and have him make plans to give you dialysis. Then, I'll come back and speak to you. If at that time you still don't want dialysis, you need to sign a paper that you are refusing treatment, and I will not admit you to the hospital. You will need to sign out of this emergency room against medical advice."

Dr. Mars went to the nursing area and asked the nephrologist on call to be paged. The nephrologist said he would come down and give the patient two hours of dialysis. Dr. Mars went back to the patient and told him.

The patient looked upset. "How come I'm getting only two hours of dialysis?" he asked. "My doctor told me that I need four hours when I start because I'm so heavy."

Dr. Mars said, "Let me see if I understand this. First, you don't want dialysis. Second, we find out you already have a shunt. Now, you don't want two hours of dialysis, you want more—the four hours that your doctor prescribed. If I were you, I would have done what your doctor told you originally, instead of waiting until you reached this condition and coming here. You are getting two hours of dialysis treatment and further treatment will depend on the nephrologist."

Dr. Mars checked his watch, and guessed from the time that the sun must be setting outside. "Actually, I'm an internist and in general medicine, but the nephrologist does not admit patients, so I'm the one admitting you. Please spare me: If you have any other questions or want to fight anymore, feel free to do it with your nephrologist. You have a good day."

As Dr. Mars turned to walk out, the patient called him back. "Hey Doc, I'm so sorry. I don't mean to give you a hard time. It looks like you're having a bad day."

Dr. Mars shook his head. "No, I'm not having a bad day. I'm just trying to help you with your predicament. It seems that you have a problem facing the facts and getting control of your life. The doctor told you that your kidney was not working. You have a shunt in your hand, ready for dialysis. When you got sick, you did not go to the hospital where you doctor knows you, you came here. I'm not having a bad day, and I'm not angry with you. I'm simply trying to help you."

As Dr. Mars left, he shook hands with the emergency room physician, got in his car, and started the engine. Before he drove away, he clicked open the glove compartment and brought out a piece of paper. He wrote on it in large, capital letters.

I AM WORKING ON A NEW BOOK. IT IS TITLED 'THE PREACHER STORY.' I AM RELYING ON INTERACTIONS WITH PEOPLE LIKE YOU TO WRITE THIS BOOK BECAUSE WE, AS HUMANS, ARE ALL PREACHERS.

He stopped there, and he thought to himself, there's no way I can give this to a patient. He crumpled the paper, opened the window to his car, and threw it into the street.

CHAPTER 3

▼

Dr. Filip Mars had a relaxing weekend, and on Monday, he arrived at the clinic before anyone else. He sat at his desk and brought out his pen and a piece of paper so he could write down his thoughts.

All I want in life is peace of mind, good health and happiness. That is prosperity to me. Money is just to pay bills. It is such a materialistic article. Money: The more you make, the more you spend. The higher you have, the higher your expenses. Peace of mind comes from satisfaction, which is what I want, and that is what I will get. What I hope for is a state of Utopia. It sounds like an imagination, but really, it is achievable.

Good health is a blessing from God. Nobody can work for it. But, you can modify the factors to stay alive in a healthy way, even in a diseased state. It is like being in a world where no harm is done to our bodily system—no accidents, no pollution. No genetics transcended from generation to generation, cursing the legs to walk on.

It is like an imagination that is very transient. One day you are healthy, another day you are not. But, who can live forever? Staying healthy at all costs remains a blessing from God. Happiness is a state of the mind. It is a way that the human has conformed and adapted to severities, both physical and mental. It's a daily way of life that sees us through the ups and downs and hard times. It is a manner in which the brain approaches an obstacle. Give or take, if we do it better, if we don't do the dance, why not be damned happy? Prosperity is wisdom.

He read what he wrote. Then he opened up his e-mail to send a message to Ben.

Hi Ben. This weekend was very tough for me. I couldn't meet with you. Can we meet tonight?

Cima Trotford, the nurse, was the first to come in. Dr. Mars called her into his office and asked her to have a seat.

"Cima, what did you think of the patient that came in the other day, my neighbor who didn't want to pay?"

Cima said that she didn't like him. "Something seemed wrong about him, and he was very arrogant, acting like he could just walk in and see the doctor at his own leisure. Also, he looked like a gay," Cima said.

"And what is wrong with being gay?" Dr. Mars asked tersely. "There is nothing wrong with being gay, that's just his sexual preference. Are you anti-gay, Cima?"

"No, I'm not," said Cima defensively.

"I think that you are," said Dr. Mars. Cima looked very uncomfortable, and she kept rubbing the wrist of her right hand with her left.

"No, I'm not. I have nothing against gays. I actually have a sister that's a lesbian. But due to our upbringing, my family doesn't encourage it."

"And what's your upbringing?" Dr. Mars asked.

"We're religious, into the Bible. We were taught that a man and women are meant to live together and make children, not two men or two women." Cima declared her beliefs proudly. Then, seeing the doctor's disapproving look, she reconsidered. "But, things change," she added. "When all of these things were written, the world was not like this. The world has become a confusing place. There were no computers, or electricity, or even running water when the Bible was written. All of the things in the Bible are not necessarily applicable to our lives."

The conversation wasn't easy for Cima, and she took the pause as an opportunity to get back to work. "Doc, I've got to go," she said. "The patients will be arriving shortly."

Dr. Mars went to his students, who by this time were waiting for him in the lounge area. "I hope you had a nice weekend" He told them. "What did you all do?"

Eva Holloway did not study anything, but she was very frank about it. "I went to see a movie, and my parents came into town to visit me for the weekend," she said.

Dr. Mars asked Mel if she had studied anything.

"Yes, I did." Mel said. "I actually took some practice tests on congestive heart failure, and I was amazed about how much I knew."

Dr. Mars asked her what she scored on the test. She said that out of ten questions, she got five right.

"That's not good," Dr. Mars teased. "You should get them all right."

"But that was the first time I took it," Mel said. "I'm not a very good test-taker—I need to take them two or three times before I can pass them."

Dr. Mars chuckled. "You make it sound like life. Life is a test—you have to do things two or three times before you can get them right."

Don cut in. "Well, this weekend was my birthday."

"Do you believe in birthdays, Don?" Dr. Mars asked.

Don looked confused. "Why not?" he asked. "It's a special day for me. I've always celebrated my birthday, even if I'm alone. My parents always call me and wish me a happy birthday. This year, I went to a restaurant with my girlfriend and had a nice time. My birthdays are very special to me."

Dr. Mars asked him, "What makes a birthday special?"

"It's the day I was born. You only get born once," Donald joked.

"I suppose," Dr. Mars said, rolling his eyes. "But I don't believe in celebrating birthdays. I believe that you need to utilize and find meaning in every day. Your birthday is just the day that you came into this world to start your struggle, and to appreciate the essence of the Almighty Being, and to contribute your own to the world. The only way you can achieve that is to utilize every single minute of every single day, and not just be happy that you were born into the world without taking charge. Be someone that has come into this world, has learned, has grown, and has been instrumental in the moving history of the human race."

Don looked as if the doctor had slapped him. "I like birthdays, too," Eva whispered to him, trying to cheer him up.

But the doctor continued with his message. "Some people celebrate a birthday for a one year old. What does that one year old know? Nothing. It's just a waste of everybody's time and money."

"But the parents are happy that their child is alive and healthy," Mel protested. "Doesn't that mean anything?"

"I don't understand what the parents are so happy about," Dr. Mars responded. "They have not trained the child; they don't know what the child will be. You should celebrate a child who has gone to school, who has been trained and gained knowledge, and who is ready to tackle the world for the well-being of other humans."

The students were silent. "Let's settle down for the day's business," Dr. Mars said.

The first patient of the day was in her thirties. She was sobbing when they walked into the room.

"Why are you crying?" Dr. Mars asked.

In between her tears she said, "I need to see a psychiatrist."

Dr. Mars asked why.

"I've been trying to kill myself." The med students looked startled. Eva looked away from the patient, focusing her eyes on the floor and hoping that the patient couldn't tell how uncomfortable she was.

"What have you done to try to kill yourself?" Dr. Mars asked.

"I've thought about taking pills like Tylenol, but I know that would just make me suffer before I died," The patient responded.

"Do you have a gun at home?" Dr. Mars asked.

"No."

"Do you have knives at home?"

"Only in the kitchen."

"Have you ever thought about slashing your throat?"

"No, maybe my wrists."

"OK, Ms. Crain, why do you want to kill yourself?"

She stared at the floor, not speaking. Eva looked back up at her, and repeated gently, "Why do you want to kill yourself, Ms. Crain?"

With tears in her eyes, she said softly, "I'm just so tired of life."

Dr. Filip Mars took a seat next to her and took her hand. "Rule number one, do not take your own life," he said. "The reason is that you are not the maker of your life. You did not give life to yourself. Your life was given to you by the Almighty God who has a plan for you to contribute to the world. What are you going to gain by getting fed up with life? Life is challenging, controlling, compelling. At times, things just don't go right. So take control and take charge of your life."

While he was talking, he looked at the patient's records and he took her vital signs. He left the medical students with her to take down her history, and then he went back in his office and wrote a recommendation for the psychiatrist. Then, he sent her to be admitted to the hospital.

Don was flustered when he left the patient's room. "Dr. Mars, why are you sending her to the hospital for admission and telling her to see a psychiatrist as soon as possible after what you just told her?"

Dr. Mars paused for a moment and said, "I don't believe in many of the things we do. This young lady is not going to do anything to herself. She won't slash her throat, she doesn't have a gun, and she won't jump from a moving train or an 18-story building. But the way the system is set up, if you don't follow the loop, that loop will be hung around your neck, and that loop will choke you."

"I still don't understand," Don said.

"For the sake of saving our licenses, we do all sorts of things, like sending this patient to the hospital," Dr. Mars said. "One of these days you are going to be faced with a patient like this, and you're going to remember that you want be able to face the judge with a leg to stand on. You don't want to be legless in the presence of the judge. You have to flow with the loop."

All the students nodded their heads, and they continued to see the next patient. New to the practice, the patient told them how many wonderful things she had heard about Dr. Mars and his unconventional "tough love" talks.

Although he seemed harsh, many of Dr. Mars' patients loved his approach. They appreciated his honest assessments, and loved that he always listened to all that they had to say and offered them practical advice. Even if they didn't take it, he still welcomed them back, but he was always realistic and never sugarcoated their conditions. Although he was unconventional, even his students seemed to understand and appreciate his approach.

At the end of that day, Dr. Mars told the students that he was going to leave the clinic early because he had to prepare for a lecture he was giving the following afternoon.

"Where is this lecture, and can we come?" Don asked.

"Of course," Dr. Mars said. "I forgot to tell you about it. It's at lunchtime tomorrow at the local mall. I'll be talking to the community about popular topics like cholesterol and diabetes management and overall well-being."

After the students left, Dr. Mars finished his paperwork and got in his sedan. But instead of heading home, he headed toward the north side of the town. He drove for close to an hour, and pulled to the side of the road near some shrubs in a deserted area. It was dusk, and his tires had kicked up a cloud of dust from the poorly paved road that hung all around his car. He waited, feeling anxious and thinking about his present symptoms. Rapid heart beat. Shortness of breath.

The red truck finally pulled up behind him, and in his rearview mirror, Dr. Mars could see Ben, even though he was wearing a large, floppy hat that almost completely covered his eyes. Ben pulled his truck around Dr. Mars' sedan, and Dr. Mars followed him down the road. In a few miles, they entered a cornfield, and the plants rose up around the cars like thousands of sentinels keeping watch over them.

They reached an area where no corn grew; stalks from past harvests lay flattened on the dirt, and tire marks in the mud signaled that the men had been there before. Dr. Mars turned his car off, and Ben left his truck in idle. Dr. Mars sat in his car for several minutes, adjusting his mirrors, rubbing his fingers on the steering wheel, and looking at that hat in the rearview mirror. He thought that it looked very stupid, and for some reason, that thought made him ashamed.

He got out of his car and walked quickly to the red truck.

"What were you waiting for?" Ben asked, running his fingers lightly across Dr. Mars' brow. Dr. Mars thought he was wearing too much rouge. Then again, any rouge was too much for him, really.

Dr. Mars did not answer. Instead, he rested his hand on Ben's thigh.

"I'm so glad to see you," Ben said, his ruby red lips glistening.

The following day, Dr. Mars seemed very happy and well rested. He told his students that he had gone out for a late dinner with his wife.

"Your wife, what's her name again?" Mel asked.

"Lucinda," he said, imagining her smooth complexion and curly, black hair.

"Can I ask you a question, doctor?" Don asked.

"Of course," Dr. Mars said.

"Many of the doctors in private practice have their wives as office managers. Why don't you?"

Dr. Mars shook his head and said, "I don't think I would like her to work with me. I love her, but I don't want to see her all the time. The office is my place for me to do my work. At home, that's our place for us to be together."

The clinic was packed, with more patients than chairs in the waiting room. Dr. Mars attended to business quickly, and by noon, he packed his notes for the lecture. He drove to the mall in his black sedan, and the three students followed him in Mel's beat up, green Chevy.

At the mall, a stage in front of hundreds of chairs had been set up in the open area where Santa's Wonderland stood in the winter. The moderator asked Dr. Mars if one of his students would like to introduce him to the crowd.

Dr. Mars gestured to Don, who could barely contain his excitement at being chosen. Don went to the podium and tapped on the microphone to get everyone's attention.

"This afternoon's lecture is going to be about general health management," Don said." I therefore introduce to you Dr. Filip Mars, whom I will refer to as the preacher."

Dr. Mars went to the podium and shook hands with Don. "That was a good introduction—we didn't even plan it," he said. As a matter of fact, Don didn't even know that this lecture would take place until yesterday I love that name, too—the preacher."

Dr. Mars looked briefly at his notes. It was the only time he used them during his entire speech. "I'm going to tell you guys a story today, and that story is about your health. It's about your environment, and what you take in and put out. It's about how to control yourself. A lot of us are now in the habit of eating like there's no tomorrow, because we believe we can get medication from our doctor to help lower our cholesterol. We eat salt, and believe that if we get high blood pressure, we can just use diuretics. Medication, medication, medication. Nobody ever talks about lifestyle."

Dr. Mars went on to explain that diuretics are not good for people's systems because they remove essential minerals in addition to the salt.

"Why not make a lifestyle change instead?" he asked the audience. As he had started speaking, even more shoppers had heard his voice booming over the speaker system. Now, more than 300 people were seated in front of the stage, listening to him.

"Eat less and avoid medications. Just watch what you eat, and don't take in too much salt."

He went on to his next topic. "What about high blood pressure? I agree that it's genetic. You get it from your parents, grandparents, and great grandparents. However, we're not helping ourselves by having a negative attitude and putting all kinds of unhealthy things into our bodies anyway. You are just eating lots of salt and putting all kinds of bad things in your body, and getting ready to start medication because your father or mother had the same problem. You have to denounce the problem and tell your own system that you don't want to follow that route. Family genetics matter, but society matters more. What you put in your body matters the most."

Dr. Mars asked the members of the audience to raise their hands if they had an established exercise routine. Only a few people raised their hands.

"You were here to shop, and didn't expect that in the middle of your afternoon, there'd be a preacher here. But here is the preacher, standing here before you, asking you what you have done to modify your lifestyle in terms of exercising. I think the answer would be nothing," Dr. Mars said. "Those of you that were able to raise your hands, I can tell you how good that is for you. You reward is not going to be in heaven—it's going to be right here on earth, because you're going to have good health."

Next, Dr. Mars spoke about cholesterol. "Almost everything we eat has cheese, yolk and fat in it. We need a little bit of cholesterol in our lives, but not as much as we eat. It's clogging our arteries and veins. Now we are all on medications to reduce cholesterol, but they are not just reducing the cholesterol, they are weakening the body. They weaken the liver and muscles. Instead, try controlling your mouth around cheese and beef burgers."

Dr. Mars saw that the crowd was paying attention, and it appeared some members of the audience were even taking notes. His med students sat in the front row, and when he made eye contact with her, Eva gave him a thumbs up.

"The common thing that kills the body is excess. When you rest too must, you rust. A lot of people sleep too much. When patients come into my clinic with insomnia, I ask them why they can't sleep. They tell me that they have slept during the day. You can't sleep during the day and sleep during the night, you have to choose one. God did not design you to sleep twice." He paused, taking a sip of water from the bottle that the moderator had left on the podium.

"When patients say they haven't slept during the day, I ask them what they were doing before they tried to go to sleep. They say they were watching TV, getting themselves all excited. Don't watch TV; pick up a newspaper or book and read. Give your brain a challenge to make it tired. Do exercise—walk, jog, run—and then take a shower. When you get to bed, you will be able to sleep. Your body is a feedback system: when you use it, when it's tired, it will sleep. Lifestyle modification and a positive attitude will give you the feedback that you desire."

He completed the lecture and answered some questions from the audience. The audience seemed impressed, and gave him a standing ovation with lots of applause.

After the lecture, the people who organized it had arranged for him to have a lunch with his students at a nearby restaurant.

"What are you going to order?" he asked them, grinning. "A salad or a beef burger?"

Eva Holloway shook her head. "I love my burgers, but I liked the lecture, too."

The last patient of the day was new to the practice. Her chart said she was 67 years old. But when Dr. Mars and the students went into the room, there were two women. One looked like she was in her eighties—very old, frail and sick. The other looked like she was in her sixties, and very healthy.

Dr. Mars took a seat across from the lady who looked older and asked her, "How old are you, ma'am?"

She said, "I'm 52 years old. But I'm not the patient."

He said, "Oh, are you her mother?"

The woman looked annoyed. "No, I'm not her mother, I'm her provider," she said.

Dr. Mars tried to downplay his misunderstanding. He turned to the patient and said, "OK, Ms. Patient, now to you!"

When he finished with the patient, he went into the corridor and asked the students, "You see these people abusing the system? The provider looks much older than the patient, and the provider is not doing anything for this patient other than just collecting money every two weeks, and it's government money."

He felt his phone vibrate in his pocket, and he checked his text messages. He replied to the person who had texted him, and put his phone back in his pocket. Then, he told the students that the next morning, they would do rounds in the hospital with him.

"See you bright and early," he said.

"Better drink some coffee," Mel muttered.

CHAPTER 4

▼

Dr. Filip Mars met with the students the next morning by the hospital's cafeteria. Mel was sipping a latte, and Don was already working on a diet soda.

He said, "Well, we're going to start rounds. I usually start on the second floor and then go over to the intensive care unit. Luckily, today I only have one patient in the intensive care unit, so we're not going to waste a lot of time there. As we go along, feel free to ask me and the patients questions."

Dr. Mars told the students that after they finished the rounds, he was going to two other, smaller hospitals to check on his patients there. "You guys can go ahead of me to the clinic, and I'll be there by the time our patients arrive," he said.

As they walked down the corridor of the hospital, they came to the elevator. Eva stopped in front of it, but Dr. Mars kept walking. Not sure what to do, Don and Mel followed after Dr. Mars. He turned back, frowning at Eva.

"Don't tell me you're going to use the elevator just to get to the second floor. We can use the stairs," he said disapprovingly.

On the second floor, they went to the nurses' station and asked for the nurse in charge. She helped them find Dr. Mars' patients' charts and place them in a cart that he could wheel to each room. He got ten charts from the charge nurse and then started down the hall, with Don pushing the cart behind him.

As they entered each room, most of the patients were still asleep. In one room, the patient was snoring with his face covered by his sheets. Dr. Mars went close to him.

"Mr. Jones, how are you doing today? I'm so sorry to be bugging you at this time of day. Are you doing OK?" Dr. Mars asked loudly.

The patient stirred, pulled the sheets from his face, and said, "Oh, its you again. I think I'm all right, but I've seen better days. I've been coughing a lot, and my temperature is going up."

Dr. Mars flipped through Mr. Jones' chart and told the students that Mr. Jones has pneumonia. "We have him on some antibiotics." He handed the chart to Mel. "Check on his chart and see if the blood culture has shown anything yet."

Mel searched the paperwork. "No, it doesn't look like we have the blood culture back yet" she said.

Dr. Mars moved close to the patient, put the stethoscope on his chest, and asked him to take deep breaths, in and out. After listening to several breaths, he asked the students if any of them would like to try listening to the patient's chest. Don quickly stepped forward and placed his stethoscope on the patient's chest in the same spot as Dr. Mars.

"What do you hear?" Dr. Mars asked.

"It looks like he has some crackles on the right side of his lung," Don said.

"Very good," Dr. Mars said. He looked up at the patient. "Mr. Jones, right now, we think you have pneumonia. It's possible however, that you might also have congestive heart failure. Since you just got in yesterday, it's too early for us to be sure."

Dr. Mars turned to Mel. "Did the gram stain grow anything yet?"

Mel flipped through the chart twice before answering, "No, not yet."

The next patient was a woman named Molly Pritchard. Dr. Mars explained to the students that she had a biopsy of her liver to check for a possible tumor.

"Is there any report back yet?" he asked the charge nurse as she stepped into the room to check on him.

"Mrs. Pritchard is being seen by gastroenterology today, and we are still waiting on the biopsy report," the nurse responded. Dr. Mars told the patient that they would wait for the results to determine if she would be discharged or not.

Closing the door behind them as they left the room, Dr. Mars spoke with the students about why the patient had been biopsied. "Mrs. Pritchard has Hepatitis C, and the GI doctor thinks it has been there for a long time, about 20 years. She has been losing a lot of weight and having some bleeding problems, which is why we think she has probably developed liver cancer."

Eva and Don exchanged sympathetic glances as they headed to the next patient's room. As they opened the door, they were surprised to find the patient, a 67-year-old woman, sitting straight up in her bed and staring at them.

"Hey, Dr. Mars!" she shouted excitedly. "Let me tell you how constipated I am. I haven't pooped in days! Your treatment isn't working."

Dr. Mars smiled and told his students, "Mrs. Greenway is here for a bowel obstruction. She's had a series of small bowel obstructions in the past, and she came in complaining of abdominal pain. We've had her on an NG tube and have been giving her mineral oil, and it appears that the obstruction has passed."

"Yeah," Mrs. Greenway cut in unabashedly. "I pooped days ago, but now nothing again!"

Dr. Mars sighed and continued. "Now we're taking out the NG tube and we've started her on a clear liquids diet." He bent over and listened to her belly. "You have very good bowel sounds, Mrs. Greenway. I don't think you're constipated. You aren't passing stool because you're on a liquid diet, and your body can't make waste when it hasn't taken in food. After a few days on liquids, we'll start you on some solid food, and then you should be able to move your bowels."

After leaving the patient's room, Dr. Mars gathered the students in the hallway and shook his head disapprovingly. "This is what I keep telling everybody. People just want medication for everything. Mrs. Greenway wants medication for constipation when she hasn't eaten for three days. She has taken so many laxatives at this point that her bowels no longer function properly, and she has chronic obstructions. This is exactly the reason that medication isn't the answer to everything."

Before entering the next room, the charge nurse asked to speak to Dr. Mars.

"We can't get Mr. Olympus' sugar down," she told him. "His glucose keeps running very high. I've been talking to endocrinology, and his sugars aren't coming down at all."

In his dimly lit room, Mr. Olympus was sleeping on his side. The huge man, who weighed more than 300 pounds, was snoring loudly. A petite blonde woman with black tattoos covering both her arms like sleeves slept quietly next to him on a cot.

"Who is that?" Mel asked, nodding her head toward the woman.

"I believe it's his girlfriend, or possibly his wife," Dr. Mars said.

"There's somebody for everyone," Eva whispered in awe. Don snorted a short laugh, and Dr. Mars shot him an angry glance.

Once inside the room, the students' expressions turned to disgust as they smelled something putrid. As Dr. Mars approached Mr. Olympus, he saw that the table near the window was covered with nearly empty boxes of pizza, French fries and fast food burgers. Crusts and cheese dribbles dotted the table, with the remnants of a half-drank chocolate shake forming a sticky pool across the boxes.

"Mr. Olympus, good morning!" Dr. Mars said in a loud, cheerful voice. The patient snorted and stirred. Finally, he turned to face the doctor. "How are you doing?" Dr. Mars asked.

"Doc, I'm doing all right," Mr. Olympus said, glancing at his girlfriend, who was still sleeping. "I'm good, but this sugar thing is just not getting under control."

Dr. Mars shook his head. "I can imagine it isn't, not with all these boxes of pizza that you've emptied into your belly and all the French fries. We're not going to be able to control your sugar if you're not dieting. You're only in your forties, and you should have a long life ahead of you, but you're eating yourself to death."

"I know, I know," Mr. Olympus said, rolling his eyes. "But I need to eat, man. My sugar is high, but the food they're giving me here isn't enough. The portions are way too small. I know I shouldn't eat as much, but they're trying to starve me to death. That's why I have to feed myself."

"And where did all this food come from, Mr. Olympus?" Dr. Mars asked. "If the nurses knew you were eating all this, they certainly wouldn't be happy."

Just then, the sleeping woman opened her eyes. She blinked, looking disoriented, and then noticed the doctor. "Hi, Doc," she said cautiously.

"Well hello," Dr. Mars said, shaking her hand warmly. "And who are you?"

"I'm Tara, Jake's girlfriend." she said. She stood up and moved over to Mr. Olympus's bed and kissed him on the forehead. "How are you, Hon?"

Before Mr. Olympus could answer, Dr. Mars asked her if she was the one bringing him all the food.

Tara blushed. "Well yes," she admitted. "But only because they're not feeding him enough, and he keeps getting hungry."

"But you are not helping us with your boyfriend's problem," Dr. Mars said. "His sugars keep running high—that's why he came into the hospital. One of these days he's going to pass out on us, and you're not going to have somebody to feed anymore. You're helping him kill himself slowly."

"No!" Tara yelped, rubbing her boyfriend's belly affectionately. "I'm not going to kill him. What are you talking about?"

"Well you're giving him so much unhealthy food that's full of carbohydrates and fat. He needs to have small meals at regular intervals, not huge, unhealthy meals all the time."

"But he's a big guy," she said defensively as she touched his belly. "He needs to eat more than the average person."

The doctor looked from Tara to Mr. Olympus, and shrugged his shoulders. "I believe we've done what we can for you, Mr. Olympus. You're going against our advice by continuing to eat like this, and I think you know what you need to do to both lose weight and lower your sugars. I'm going to discharge you and schedule you another appointment with a dietician." Dr. Mars glanced at Eva. "Check Mr. Olympus' chart and tell me what his last sugar was, please."

Eva took the chart from Don, who had been examining it as Dr. Mars spoke with the patient. "It was 215 yesterday," Eva said.

"See?" Tara said excitedly. "That's not bad for him."

"Really?" Don asked.

"Yeah, he runs 400 and 500 easy," Tara said. "Looks like he's doing good!"

Dr. Mars didn't comment. "I'm keeping you on insulin, and I'd like you to come see me in the clinic after you see the dietician," the doctor told Mr. Olympus. "Do you have any questions?"

"Sure. What can I eat now?" Mr. Olympus asked.

Dr. Mars could barely contain his annoyance. "Mr. Olympus, we've been over this several times, and you will go over it again with the dietician. You ask me this every time I see you, and I still have the same answer for you. Avoid food with high carbohydrates and high sugar. That means no sodas, no milkshakes—certainly, none of the food you have here," he said, pointing at the foul-smelling table. "Eat more vegetables and salads. Do not eat heavy meals in one sitting. Try eating small meals at regular intervals."

"OK, Doc," Mr. Olympus said with a sarcastic tone. "On my honor as a boy scout, I'll try."

Dr. Mars shook his hand and said, "OK, then I'll see you soon, Comrade."

Outside the room, Dr. Mars shrugged and looked sadly at the students. "With patients like Mr. Olympus, you just have to keep giving the same message and reinforcing it. He may never listen, but at least as a doctor, you've done your best. A lot of people like him believe they should eat, drink and be merry, for tomorrow, everybody shall die." He took Mr. Olympus' chart from Eva, and tapped it with his pen. "Unfortunately, they're right—someday, they will die, and due to their unhealthy habits, it will probably be sooner than their friends."

When they finished rounds, Dr. Mars took the students down to the intensive care unit. His patient was intubated and on mechanical ventilation. Dr. Mars made some adjustments to his medication and asked the charge nurse to page him if there were any updates. Then, he told the students to have some breakfast and meet him in the clinic in an hour.

"When will you have breakfast?" Eva asked the doctor, sounding like a concerned mother.

Dr. Mars chuckled. "I know it's against doctor's orders, but I usually don't have breakfast. I'll have some coffee on the way to the office, though."

The students left, and Dr. Mars visited two other hospitals before arriving early at the clinic. A full hour before the clinic officially opened, Dr. Mars could see from the inside of the receptionist's window that one patient was already seated in the waiting room. It was Ben.

This time, Ben was dressed even more conspicuously as a woman. His hair was pulled back in a pink clip, and he was wearing a pale pink blouse baring his thin, flat stomach. His legs were shaved and covered in some sort of sparkling lotion, which Dr. Mars noticed because he was wearing a ripped denim skirt that, when seated, came only to the middle of his thighs.

Before he could react, Cima rushed up to the doctor. "Your *friend* is back, and he said he needs to talk to you. I asked him if he had any problems and he said he's been passing out," she said. "I didn't know what to do with him. You said to let you know before I put him in an exam room—but do you really want your other patients to see a man like this in your office?

Dr. Mars looked uncomfortable and distressed. "All right, just put him in my private office," he muttered.

Cima went to the waiting area and took Ben into the office, while Dr. Mars went to the break room to collect his students. Patients started arriving, and his nurses were busy putting charts together and placing patients in exam rooms to check their vital signs.

Dr. Mars was so busy lecturing the students on some of the patients they had seen that morning that he forgot Ben was waiting for him. Cima came to remind him, and he excused himself from the medical students and went into his office, slamming the door behind him. After a few minutes, he came out and asked Cima to check Ben's blood sugar.

"Is he diabetic?" Cima asked.

"Who knows," Dr. Mars said. "He is worrying himself so much, I'm just going to check it to be sure there's nothing wrong."

Angel Gold passed by, a cup of coffee in one hand and a stack of charts in the other. She frowned. "From the looks of it, he doesn't need his sugar checked. He needs an HIV test."

Dr. Mars' eyes got wide, and he furrowed his brow. "It's unlike you to say such a thing, Angel. He's my neighbor. Why would he need to be checked for HIV? Just because he's gay doesn't mean he needs to be checked for HIV."

The med students, who had been blocking Angel Gold's way in the hall, moved aside for her to pass. "Well, HIV is more common in gay people, and this is clearly a gay guy," Mel said.

Dr. Mars responded tonelessly. "That's incorrect, Mel. HIV is no longer more common in the gay population. It's unfair of you to judge someone and make a diagnosis based purely on his sexual preference."

"Sorry," Mel said quickly, looking down at her shoes.

Cima went in and checked Ben's sugar. Coming out of the room, Dr. Mars saw her frown and shake her head. The students also seemed uncomfortable with the situation, and began discussing the morning's patients' records in order to change the topic. Dr. Mars looked sternly at Cima, and asked to see her alone in the break room.

"Your friend's sugar is only 85," Cima told him once they were alone. "What would you like me to do with him now?"

Dr. Mars looked Cima straight in the eyes, and said slowly to her, "Do you have a problem with this patient, Cima?"

Cima started to say no. Then, with a rush of emotion, she changed her answer. "I don't have a problem with him, personally. If he wants to dress like a woman and come in here acting silly, that's his choice. I do think, though, that he needs to start paying when he comes to visit, just like any other patient. You're giving him preferential treatment, allowing him to sit in your private office. He calls you by your first name, and that's just disrespectful. And it seems obvious to me that he's not just coming in here because of his health. You should be careful, doctor. You don't know what is going on in his strange head."

Dr. Mars tried to keep his composure. He took several deep breaths before responding. "Cima, calm down," he said, touching her shoulder. "Don't let this work you up. It's true that my friend is unusual, but he's perfectly harmless. I just want to help him as much as I possibly can. However, you're right—he should not get preferential treatment in front of my other patients. I'll speak with him and let him know he can't continue coming in without making an appointment and setting up a payment plan."

Cima seemed satisfied, and Dr. Mars felt assured that he had the situation under control. He walked into his office and spoke with Ben. Despite his hushed tones, the students and nurses couldn't help but hear Ben's angry voice from behind the closed door. They just couldn't make out what he was saying.

Before leaving his office, Dr. Mars ran his fingers through his hair, adjusted his white coat, and took several more deep breaths. He led Ben out the front door of the clinic without speaking. With the door shut and Ben out of hearing range in the parking lot, he declared in front of the patients in the waiting room, "What a troubled young man. I will see what I can do to help him. I'm so glad this troubled young soul has come and trusted me enough to share his problems with me."

A patient peeking over the top of her magazine made eye contact with the doctor, and nodded supportively. Yes, her nod seemed to say. You are such a kind, trustworthy man.

The day went by quickly, and Dr. Mars saw almost twice as many patients as usual. Since his talk at the mall, several new patients had set up appointments, saying that they were looking for a doctor who would help them make healthy life changes and become less dependant on medications.

When Dr. Mars left the clinic, he headed again for the north side of town. Again, he drove through the cornfields, and thought to himself that the plants already seemed taller and sturdier than they had just days earlier.

Ben was waiting in his truck, and Dr. Mars followed him to their usual spot. As he drove, a clammy sweat broke out on his large hands. He was strangely serene as he wiped away the sweat, calmed by the consistency of the rows of corn.

Parked in the clearing, Dr. Mars climbed into Ben's truck. Ben was dressed the same as he had been earlier in the day, but his makeup was ruined. His blotchy eye shadow and smeared mascara brought even more attention to his masculine features. He had sharp cheekbones and a cleft chin, and his eyebrows were bushy and too large.

"You were a jerk today," Ben told him angrily.

"I was not. It is simply a matter of fact that you can't come in to my clinic anymore. It's too suspicious, Ben," the doctor replied.

"Oh really?" Ben asked, pouting. "You don't seem to think it's too suspicious to fuck me in the middle of this cornfield, where Mr. Farmer on his tractor might come by at any moment. Maybe I shouldn't come here, either."

"Be quiet," Dr. Mars said, He put his hand on the back of Ben's head, and pushed his mouth gently toward his. Then, more firmly, he pushed it lower.

As Dr. Mars was driving home, it began to rain heavily. Lightning came next, with loud thunder that almost shook the car. He barely heard the trill of his phone over the sounds of the storm. Flipping it open he saw a message.

I'm already missing you.

Dr. Mars shook his head, and texted back with one hand as the other guided the steering wheel.

You're crazy. I just saw you.

Their relationship had been this way since their first meeting almost a year ago. When Dr. Mars took his sedan to a local car shop to have a scratch buffed out, he didn't pay much attention to the feminine mechanic in his baggy workman's shirt, his scraggly hair pulled back with a simple rubber band. But Ben saw something in Dr. Mars.

"Here's my card. You call me if you ever need anything," Ben had said, brushing Dr. Mars' palm for just a moment too long. When the doctor pulled the card from his pocket later that night, alone in his study while he wife was sleeping, he saw that it wasn't a card. It was a slip of sturdy paper, with a message scrawled in script: "Please call me."

The next morning as he drove to work, Dr. Mars called the number written below the words. That night, he met Ben in the cornfield. Ben was dressed as a woman, and spoke to Dr. Mars with the tone and attitude of a petulant child. Dr. Mars found his womanly masquerade annoying, and his talk of covert love affairs and secret rendezvous incredibly naïve. Still, for the first of the hundreds of times to come, he let Ben satisfy him that night in a way that his wife had never been able to do—a way that he hadn't experienced since he married her and swore to stop sleeping in sin with men.

Once he pulled into his garage, Dr. Mars pulled a small tin from his glove compartment. He shook several mints into his mouth, chewed them quickly, and went into his house. He passed through his living room, a huge space decorated beautifully and filled with accessories, fine furniture and a state-of-the art television. He went to his bedroom, and noticed with a start that the lights and television were still on.

For a moment, he thought that his wife might still be awake, and he prepared an excuse for her. "Honey, I'm so sorry. We have so many new patients, and I spent all night dictating their histories and getting their files in order."

But Dr. Mars didn't need his excuse. His wife, Lucinda, was sleeping quietly on her stomach, her long, curly black hair spread wildly across her pillow. Her tiny, manicured fingers gripped the sheets around her, and a tiny smile was spread across her delicate, pretty face.

The doctor tried to be quiet as he walked through the room, but Lucinda was a light sleeper. She turned onto her back and blinked sleepily at him.

"Hi, honey. I'm so tired—I must have fallen asleep while watching TV. Have you had dinner?"

"No," Dr. Mars said. "You know I don't like to eat late. I have to get up early, so I'll have a big breakfast. I have so many patients to see tomorrow. He bent over Lucinda and kissed her on the forehead.

"You shouldn't work so hard, Filip," she said. Then, she turned her back to him, and he shut off the lamp and television before going into the living room. He stood there in the dark, thinking and clenching his hands. He felt as if he had eaten a huge dinner—his stomach felt full, and painful cramps washed over him. Something was wrong, he thought. Something had been wrong for a long time, and it wasn't Lucinda's fault. A good woman, from a good home. An excellent pedigree—a hardworking, God-fearing woman who never missed church on Sundays and trusted him without question.

Where had he gone wrong?

He went into his room again, changed out of his clothes, and walked into his study. He switched on the light and sat in front of his cherry wood desk. Picking up a pen and paper, he started writing, the words pouring from his fingers before they even registered in his mind.

Cornfield. The grains. Yellow, white, red steaks. White floaters, flowing with the wind. All there. Sun dance. Cow's dung. The smell of rotting here. The cattle rearer smiled. The air smells familiar, and I smiled, too. The wind came. He had no teeth. I had no head to think why he is toothless. He said something to me in a language that I don't understand. I nodded my head like I did. Yes, I smell the grass. He said something to me again, and went on his knees and bowed his head to the ground. I looked all around me, and there was nobody else but me, him, the cornfield, and the grass. Was he listening to the grass?

CHAPTER 5

▼

The next morning, Dr. Mars had time to sit and chat with his students because the first patients of the day were running very late.

He said to the students, "What are you planning to do when you graduate? Do you think you'll go into private practice, work in an office with multiple doctors, or choose the hospital setting?"

Eva responded first. "I'd love to be in private practice, but it looks busy."

Don also said he would like to go into private practice, but Mel said she'd prefer to be in a hospital.

"That way, I know when I'm done for the day, I'm done. If I've signed out on my patients and I'm not on call, they won't bother me," she said.

"It's true—private practice is a lot of work," Dr. Mars said. "For example, last night I was so lucky—the hospital's paging system was down for about four hours. For six good hours, my beeper didn't go off and I was able to rest very well. It was a kind of freedom that you don't often get when you're on call all the time."

Dr. Mars heard footsteps behind him, and he turned around. His receptionist, Martha, was standing behind him. She asked him a question about the billing for one of his morning patients and then walked back to the front of the office.

Dr. Mars reflected on M&M's cheerful attitude for a moment. "I'm incredibly lucky to have such a good office manager," he told the students. "But even with someone like M&M, the major thing you have to realize is that in private practice, medicine is business. If you don't know how to manage your business, your practice won't thrive. Even the best office manager needs to be well supervised, and you have to keep track of your overhead, the running cost of your practice.

Insurance's reimbursements to doctors are dismally poor, so if you don't watch your overhead, you won't make any money."

"It sounds like it's tough to balance good patient care and good business practices, Don said sympathetically. Dr. Mars nodded.

"But aren't there companies you can hire to manage the business aspects of your practice for you?" Eva asked. Dr. Mars shook his head emphatically.

"There are, but you don't want to use them. When you have someone else managing for you, you fail to keep track of the important details, like how much money you have collected. You have to pay these companies, and as long as they get paid, they don't care how well your practice does. They only care about their own bottom line. So your bottom line should be, if you want to be in private practice, you need to know how to manage money."

Dr. Mars went on about management companies. "I've been with a practice where they used one of these companies," he said. "They don't interview potential employees well, and they end up employing incompetent people. It's better to screen the nurses and office employees yourself, to make sure that they mesh well with you and your philosophies and procedures. An outside company doesn't know your routine, and firing bad employees is tough, because they always try to retaliate by saying you're unfair."

Mel asked Dr. Mars if he had ever had a problematic employee.

"Of course I have," he said. "But my main concern wasn't her retaliation—it was that I knew she was preventing me from treating as many patients as I could because she was slowing down my system." He paused for a moment, listening as someone opened the front door to the clinic. Perhaps a patient had finally arrived.

"A quick example," he said as he stood. The students stood as well. "A couple of years back, I went to an interview with an internist in Wisconsin. He took me to three different clinics an hour away from each other. He managed all those clinics himself, so I asked him why he had multiple locations. He told me, 'Because if I don't, somebody else will.'"

"I don't understand," Mel said.

"So, the point is, to do well in private practice, you need to see as many patients as you can. He did it by having three clinics. I don't want multiple locations, so I make a point to go to three different hospitals, because the more patients I see, the more likely I am to make enough money to break even."

As they walked to the front of the clinic, Dr. Mars stopped in the middle of the hallway and turned to face the students.

"My last piece of advice for now is that in private practice, you should treat your competition as the enemy. Don't make friends with them. If you do, they'll get close to you just so that they can find your jugular. They're just pretending to be nice so they can steal your patients and copy your techniques. I stay on my own and relate to other physicians only in the lunchroom. Remember that at times, you have to be defensive."

The doctor looked at Eva, who seemed only capable of being friendly to everyone. "The saying of turning the other cheek when someone hits you—it doesn't work like that in private practice. A lot of people think the Bible is telling us to be a moron and a glutton for punishment. But I think—in private practice—if somebody hits your right cheek, don't turn your left. Go for their jugular."

"Private practice sounds scary," Eva responded. "Maybe I will change my mind."

Angelina Golden took a few steps into the hallway and announced that his patients were ready to be seen.

Before they entered the first patient's room, Dr. Mars warned the students to prepare for a heavy smell. Not sure what to expect, they were surprised when upon opening the door, they were hit with the overwhelming, cloying scent of lavender.

"Hi John, how are you doing today?" Dr. Mars asked. "John Atkins has severe asthma," he told his students.

"Oh, I'm the same," John said. "I'm still having a lot of coughing and wheezing."

"I told you, John, these perfumes are killing you!" Dr. Mars said jokingly. The students, however, knew he was serious—they realized that the smell was Mr. Atkins' cologne.

"Your asthma is aggravated by all the cologne that you wear," Dr. Mars told him.

He listened to the patient's chest and asked if he was using any medication. John said no, and Dr. Mars said, "OK, we'll see you in three months."

The day went by quickly again, and at lunchtime, Dr. Mars' telephone beeped just as he was sending his students on break. There was a text message from Ben.

Check your e-mail.

The doctor was slightly worried, and he told his students that he would see them after lunch. Dr. Mars went to his office, closed the door and opened his e-mail.

Dear Dr. Mars,

I saw your wife last night at a restaurant. You can't miss her. She's such a lovely, nice looking lady. I would like to tell you at this point that I have evidence of our love-making together. I have made several tapes using a hidden camera in my truck. You want to see one?

There was a video clip attached to the e-mail. Dr. Mars clicked on the video clip. He saw two men, one on top of the other. The man on top turned his head, and it was clear that is was Dr. Mars.

He closed the video clip quickly. He was trembling and sweating. He kept reading the e-mail.

You are very popular, doctor. You don't want anything like this getting out around town. I am demanding a sum of one million U.S. dollars. I will give you all the tapes in my possession and promise never to contact you again. This is not blackmail. I am not bullshitting you. I have legitimate reasons for needing the money. You're a doctor, and you will make it back in less than a year. All I want is the money. Remember, I did not bring you into this. You brought yourself.
   Thank you,
   Your buddy, Ben.

Dr. Mars quickly deleted the e-mail. He stared at the ceiling of his office, trying to slow down his pounding heart with long, deep breaths. Instead, he realized he was hyperventilating. I'm going to kill him, he thought. He sent Ben a message, clenching his teeth as he pressed send.
   When can we meet?
Dr. Mars got up and locked his office door. Then, he reached into his desk drawer, pulling out the top tray that held his papers and office supplies. Below it, there was a large briefcase with a combination lock. He thought for a moment, entered the combination, and opened the briefcase. In it was a .22 Magnum pistol and a bottle of vodka.

Without taking the pistol out of the case, Dr. Mars ran his fingers along its barrel. The gun had been a gift from his father when he moved to Texas, "to protect yourself from those crazy Americans." The vodka has also been a present, this one from a well-meaning but misinformed patient who didn't realize Dr. Mars didn't drink.

He had never used either of them.

Dr. Mars unscrewed the metal cap on the vodka bottle, put it to his lips, and took a long swig. Slamming the bottle down on his desk, he started to cough.

The vodka burned his throat and nostrils, and made him feel lightheaded almost instantly. He forced himself to take a few more swigs, and the placed the vodka back into the briefcase. He locked the briefcase, replaced his desk tray, and reached into his pocket for a piece of gum.

The doctor felt exhausted. He looked at his watch. The students would be coming back from lunch soon, and his heart began pounding again when he realized that they might smell alcohol on him. He spit his piece of gum into the trash and pulled a bag of cashews out of another desk drawer. He emptied half the bag into his mouth, chewed and swallowed, and put in a second piece of gum.

Before he went back to the break room, he checked his cell phone to see if Ben had responded to his text. He hadn't.

The rest of the afternoon seemed to take forever. Dr. Mars felt sluggish and hung-over, even though he hadn't been drunk. He looked pale and uncomfortable, and kept clutching his head in his large hands. After seeing two more patients, he told the nurses they needed to reschedule the others because he had a migraine. He dismissed the medical students, who seemed simultaneously concerned and happy to have the rest of the day off.

Dr. Mars felt both burning hot and chilled. He called his wife and told her that he would be coming home quite late. He checked his phone, but Ben never responded.

He waited until his nurses and receptionist left, and then he locked himself in his office, sat down in his padded chair, and closed his eyes. He dreamt of the video clip from the e-mail. In his dream, Ben's truck was on fire. Dr. Mars could see the flames surrounding them, but he couldn't stop what he was doing to save himself. Then, the flames disappeared, and instead the car was surrounded by people he knew. His wife. His students. His patients, obese and constipated and asthmatic. All were looking shocked at the preacher's terrible secret.

When Dr. Mars woke up, he didn't know what time it was. His fluorescent lights were still on, but parting the blinds behind him, he saw that it was dark outside. He stood up and instantly felt very nauseated. He ran down the corridor to the bathroom, but even though he wretched, he couldn't throw up. He washed his face, went back to his computer, and opened up his e-mail. He pulled up the deleted mail file and restored Ben's message.

He tried, but he couldn't look at it again. He picked up his cell phone and called Ben. After three tries, Ben didn't answer. He looked for a piece of paper and brought out a pen. His mind raced as he wrote.

We are like shrubs. We are like grass. Are we really humans? The other day, I was in my backyard and I saw him. He was running around, all over. Of course, on the green grass. Some have brown patches. Oh my god, some are turning real, real yellow. All in my eyes, for I am colorblind to black, purple, red and indigo. But of course, greens are best, I can make them out. And I saw him running, yes, running on the grass. My grass, which I have spent so much time invigorating by watering it, which I have put all my energy on.

Then I thought, do you really own the grass? Him, not I. Maybe me, maybe not. When we tend to the grass, we cannot wait for it, we cannot give it the life. We can sow it, and we can water it. We cannot repeat, because it's not profitable. Yes, not profitable.

I said to the grass growers, who go from dawn to dawn selling grass, "Then why do we want to own it? Why should we want to mow the grass?" And I looked at him again. I saw him fall on the grass. I was going to pick him up, but it appeared he was listening to something on the ground. He had his two hands up with his ears to the grass. Then, I paused. I did not want to go pick him up because he was at peace with what he was doing. I went back to my seat, and asked myself, "Was he into the grass?"

CHAPTER 6

▼

Dr. Filip Mars was late to work the next morning, but he appeared well rested and composed. He was dreading lunch, however, because his receptionist had arranged for him to have a catered meal with his students and his wife, who had asked him to meet the students he spoke so often about.

After a few hours of seeing patients, Cima called Dr. Mars to the nurses' station.

"Your friend is on the phone," she said. "He says he has a fever and wants to know what he can take. He says he needs to come in and see the doctor."

Dr. Mars grabbed the phone from Cima and pressed the hold button. The line was dead—Ben had hung up. "What the hell is wrong with him?" Dr. Mars muttered angrily.

Cima took his question literally, and seemed taken aback by his cursing. "Like I said, he said he has a fever, and he needs us to prescribe something. I told him he needs to make an appointment to see you because we can't prescribe anything over the phone. Maybe he's on his way for another one of his unannounced visits."

"As soon as he gets here, let me know," Dr. Mars said. "I asked him not to come in without an appointment, but if he shows up anyway, I would like to see him."

Less than an hour later, Cima shouted Dr. Mars' name down the hallway. "Your friend is on the phone *again*," she said. "I think he's crying."

Dr. Mars picked up the phone. "Hello?" Once again, Ben had hung up.

"Maybe he wants to you make a house call," Cima joked.

Dr. Mars forced laughter. "You know I don't do house calls," he said. "He needs to come in if he wants to be seen."

At lunchtime, Lucinda joined the students and her husband. Her long, curly hair was pulled half up with a large blue clip that matched her flowing blue sundress. The students thought she was very beautiful and intelligent.

"You're a lucky man," Ben told Dr. Mars. "I guess it's true that behind every good man there's a good woman."

The doctor didn't respond. He seemed very distracted, and kept fiddling with his cell phone in his pocket. Finally, he felt it vibrate, and he pulled it out of his perfectly white coat.

Check your e-mail.

Dr. Mars shook his head. Ben is crazy, and I'm going to deal with him, he thought.

Angel Gold started a conversation with Mrs. Mars. The two had talked many times over the years that Angel had been Dr. Mars' nurse.

"You know, your neighbor is very strange," Angel said. "Your neighbor who dresses like a woman. He's been calling the office and he's kind of insane."

Lucinda looked at her. Her face was blank. "My neighbor who dresses like a woman?" she repeated. "Who is that?"

"His name is Ben," Angel said. "Dr. Mars has been helping him for free."

Cima spoke up. "He's been calling the office all day, crying that he has a fever."

Lucinda stared at Cima, not breaking the glance until Cima felt uncomfortable and finally looked away. Lucinda was careful not to look at her husband.

"I don't know which neighbor you're talking about," she said, finally. "We don't have a gay neighbor. We don't have any neighbor named Ben. Most of our neighbors are old—we live in a retirement community. None of them are sick, to my knowledge."

Dr. Mars cut in, speaking quickly. "No, ladies, he's actually not our neighbor. I just didn't want to waste your time with all the details. I actually know him from one of the places where I take my car."

Cima and Angel Gold exchanged worried glances. They didn't like the look on the doctor's face.

"I need to go check my e-mail," Dr. Mars said suddenly, and he left the break room table. In his office, he read the newest message from Ben.

I am sick. I have a fever. I need this money. I am not pretending. Do you want to see another video?

Attached was another video clip. Dr. Mars did not open it.

Give me the one million bucks, and all of this will go away. I have three videos to give you. When can we meet?

Dr. Mars punched the keys on his cell phone.
Meet me tonight at our usual place. 7 p.m. I will be there, God willing.
He went back to the lunchroom, and Lucinda was getting ready to leave. She kissed Dr. Mars quickly on the forehead and reminded him that he was supposed to give a lecture at their church the upcoming Sunday.

"I remember," Dr. Mars said. "I know that I'm their hero, and I won't disappoint them."

When Lucinda left, she passed through the waiting area. A patient greeted her and asked if she was the doctor's wife. When she said yes, another patient chimed in, and both gave Dr. Mars compliments. "He is such a good man, a family man. He's so wonderful—he has the healing touch. He cares and cares for all of us."

When Dr. Mars was finished with his patients for the day, he went to his private office and pulled out his lecture materials for the Christian group on Sunday. On the top of the first paper in bold, he had written, "Diabetes, the community and you."

He made some notes on the papers, checked his watch, and left the office. In his sedan, he began the long trip toward the cornfield. We will discuss things and make this situation work, Dr. Mars thought. Or, I will strangle him.

Once at the clearing, Dr. Mars waited for Ben for half an hour. He texted him.
I am still waiting. I am by the cornfield.
Ben didn't answer. Dr. Mars tried calling him, but he got no response. The silence in his car felt like a terrible pressure, and he imagined her was in a poison gas chamber. After an hour, he drove home. He knew exactly how to remove the poison from his life.

Once home, Dr. Mars went directly to his bedroom, where Lucinda was already sleeping in a silky purple nightgown. He shook her shoulder softly. "Lucinda, can we talk?"

She looked worried, but she nodded without speaking. Still wearing his suit and tie, Dr. Mars lay down by her side and kissed her cheek.

"Lucinda, I have a confession to make."

"I know," she said. She began to cry.

"You do?" he asked.

"Yes. I think you have a gay lover, Filip."

Hearing the words from his wife, Dr. Mars began to cry as well. Lucinda spoke calmly despite the wetness collecting on her cheeks.

"I know what's been going on," she said. "A woman knows when her husband is unfaithful. And when I found pictures of naked men in your drawer, I knew you were bisexual."

Dr. Mars' tongue felt like it was pasted to his teeth. It was hard to speak, but he forced his mouth to form the words. "Then why didn't you say anything?"

"I refused to destroy this marriage based on doubts and accusations," she said. "I knew you would confess to me in time. Today, at the clinic, I could tell there was something going on between you and this gay friend. You would not lie to your staff and tell them he's our neighbor for no reason."

"It's true," Dr. Mars said tonelessly. "He's the one."

Lucinda seemed too calm to Dr. Mars. He wanted to shake her, to force her to hit him or curse at him. Instead, she took his hand and gently stroked it as she spoke. "You have betrayed this marriage, Filip. As much as you are principled, as much as you have been wonderful and helpful to your patients, you have disrespected the sanctity of our marriage by sleeping with a man. But though I am very sad for myself, I am sadder for you. You have fallen from God's grace, and it is my responsibility to bring you back to the Bible, to help you hold on to the Lord. I have prayed for him to strengthen me and you."

Lucinda's religious words disturbed Dr. Mars even more, and he began to sob audibly. He gripped his wife's hand tightly and kissed her forehead. "Darling, I'm not bisexual," he said. "Until I met you, I had always been gay. I did not ask for this. I tried to ignore my desires. But then, I found you, and I married you not only to look normal to society, but because I loved you. You are the only woman that has ever aroused me sexually."

Lucinda blushed behind her tears. She did not like to talk about sex. "I prayed for God to change me, and to give me the strength to marry you. He did, and you have made me so happy. But then, the Devil tempted me, Lucinda. He brought me to Ben, and even though he struck me as evil, I did not heed the warning."

Lucinda stopped crying. She looked deeply into her husband's eyes. "I love you. I will always, no matter what," she said. "Whether you are bisexual or gay, it doesn't matter. God has made you for me. I will stay with you. I will pray for you. And we will conquer."

She held his hand in hers, and he took her into the study room. He switched on the computer and opened the e-mail from Ben.

She read the e-mails. She did not watch the videos. "We will conquer," she repeated. "I will personally get the videotapes from this man. I will do everything to save this marriage and teach him a lesson from God for both of us. We are meant for each other. You are not supposed to be with men, you are supposed to be with me. Together, we will make this work."

Lucinda asked for Ben's phone number, and Dr. Mars wrote it down for her. "I will call him and make an appointment with him," she said. "I can handle myself. He may think he's a woman, but he's not a true woman. I am—heart, body and soul—and I will deal with this with the grace that only a true woman has."

Both husband and wife had cried so much that they couldn't any more. Instead, they just looked wearily at one another. Dr. Mars took Lucinda's hand again and led her back to the bedroom. And he said to her, "I am counting on you to track down this bastard before he puts me in the trenches."

CHAPTER 7

▼

After the service on Sunday, most of the members of the Mars' congregation stayed to hear Dr. Mars give his speech. Lucinda introduced her husband, who was wearing a bright blue suit with a white shirt and red tie. His cufflinks glistened with small diamonds. The way he smiled, no one in the congregations could have guessed the torture and pain he was going through.

"I would like to introduce to you a speaker who is very well-known in the community as a physician of great candor who reaches his patients by preaching healthy living to them," Lucinda said. "People call him the preacher. I call him my husband. Would you like to know the name that I call him? It's Honey."

Everyone laughed and applauded as he came to the podium and starting speaking with a commanding voice.

"Glucose control is very important. Diabetes is ruining us; it's the bane of our time. We carry diabetes from generation to generation. So how do you remove this label and stop the cycle? It's very easy. First, be positive. Stop being negative and believing that because diabetes has affected your mother and father, it must affect you. You have to break the chain of diabetes in your life. You need to wake up in the morning and pray that you want to break the chain. Diabetes is a killer. It can affect your sight, your legs, and your kidneys. You need to stop this course and tell diabetes, 'I will conquer you.'"

While Dr. Mars spoke to his congregation, his wife stood just outside the entrance of the church. She called Ben and made plans to meet him at a restaurant later that evening. He told her he was happy that her husband had been honest with her and that she was willing to help.

At the end of Dr. Mars' long talk, the members of the congregation gave him a standing ovation. Lucinda stood next to him and he kissed her in front of everyone.

At the car, he told her he had to go to the office to catch up on paperwork. He drove her home, and she said she was going to get some rest before meeting Ben that night. She asked Dr. Mars not to come, and he felt too weak and ashamed to refuse to let her go alone.

Dr. Mars drove to his office, muttering to himself the whole way. "Lord, give me strength. I am too arrogant to face this. Something is telling me this bastard will screw things up."

As he entered the clinic, he felt a rush of nausea. He ran into the bathroom and tried to throw up, but nothing came out. I am Dr. Filip Mars, he thought. Strong, virile, sturdy, intelligent, and a complete failure. He looked at himself in the mirror and said quietly, "I'm going to get this bastard."

Somehow, Dr. Mars knew that the meeting tonight between Ben and his wife would not come to a favorable conclusion. Ben was desperate, intent on blackmail.

Dr. Mars washed his face with cold water, accidentally splashing most of it on the mirror. He paced up and down the corridor, and thought about going public with his sexuality to keep Ben from harassing him.

"Ladies and gentlemen, I have been living a lie. I haven't practiced what I preached," he said to the corridor wall, trying out his speech for the public. But he couldn't go through with that. He would lose his career, and even if some people were encouraging of him coming out and didn't care that he was gay, he would never be taken seriously in his field again.

He sighed. He could go to the police and confess his problem. But in such a small town, the police were sure to talk, and nothing would be kept secret for long. Then information would leak in the community, and people would know what he had been doing with a man.

Dr. Mars pulled the tray from his drawer and opened the briefcase. He started gulping vodka, and had another rush of nausea . This time, he didn't go to the bathroom. He held his stomach and thought, this is the beginning of the end, but I'm not going down without a fight. I am going to make sure that I kill this bastard.

He sat up in his chair and rocked back and forth. He placed his gun in his lap, and practiced holding his finger on the trigger.

He thought that no matter what happened, he would be ridiculed in the community that he had been so devoted to. His favorite patients would turn on him and turn away from his teachings, all because of his poor choices. If he killed Ben, no one would suspect him. If he killed Ben, no one would care, either. The police probably wouldn't even investigate the death of such a ridiculous, sad man.

Dr. Mars realized with sudden certainty that Ben must be a prostitute. He must have a whole chain of men that he slept with for money, and he had simply given Dr. Mars a temporary loan. Now, he wanted to collect from his richest client.

Dr. Mars paced the hallway, sipping from the vodka bottle. Another rush of nausea came, and he held his stomach and yelled, "Ben, I will get you!"

He went back to his desk and dozed for a while. When he woke, he went to the bathroom and washed his face. He put the vodka bottle back in its case, but left the gun on his desk. He picked up his pen and wrote.

Disgrace. I went into her room. She was standing by the water basin, brushing her teeth. I was fumbling with my papers, almost wrinkling them up while waiting for her. She's taking her sweet time to brush. I didn't want to leave, because then she would think nobody came to check on her. And I looked out the window. I saw the lawn. The green lawn. The green grass. It looked so beautifully cut short, with nicely shaped hedges. I felt the nape of my neck, just like the cut of my hair. I can feel it, but probably not as nicely cut as the grass I'm looking at. I took a look at her again. She kept brushing her teeth and looking in the mirror. I looked at the mirror, too, and there it is: the image of the lawn. The green grass. It's right there, as she rinsed her mouth, slowly but surely. She is getting finished. Then she turned to me and said, "How nice of you to wait for me. I am happy to be here. Even if I am in a mental home, I don't feel sick. I am the grass." She said, "I wanted to say, I was listening to the grass."

Dr. Mars wiped tears from his eyes as he finished writing. He felt so lonely, and he said to himself, "Why me? Why did I stoop so low just to listen to the grass?"

CHAPTER 8

▼

When it got dark, Lucinda drove quickly to the restaurant where she planned to meet Ben. She asked the hostess if anyone had come to see her, and when the answer was no, she requested a table for two. While waiting to be seated, she was very nervous. She didn't even know what Ben looked like.

She sat by the window and browsed through the menu. The wine list didn't interest her—she didn't drink alcohol. She chose a salad and a diet tea. Ben didn't come.

After nearly an hour, it started raining very heavily. Lightning lit up the sky as Lucinda checked her wristwatch. She tried calling Ben, but he didn't answer.

She called her husband and asked if he had any other number for Ben. Dr. Mars sounded very tired; even Lucinda could tell he had been drinking. He said tearfully, "I don't have any other number for you. That asshole will not show up. He's after my jugular. He's going to kill me."

Mrs. Mars was worried about her husband's condition. She told him she would wait a few more minutes and then come home. "Please, don't do anything stupid, Filip," she begged. "This guy will not get us. We will conquer."

Lucinda waited another ten minutes and then called Ben again. When he didn't answer, she paid her bill and left the restaurant. In the parking lot, it was raining so heavily that she couldn't find where she parked her car. Drenched in the rain, she finally remembered she could use the panic alarm on her keys to find her car. As she approached the honking vehicle, she saw a man wearing a black raincoat.

"Lucinda, how are you?" the man asked.

"Ben?" she asked cautiously. He nodded. "You made me nervous," she sputtered. Ben was dressed all in black, with his hair pulled up in a cap so that she couldn't tell it was long. He did not seem like a frightening man. He also didn't seem like a woman.

Not sure what to do, Lucinda held out her hand. Ben shook it.

"Can we go in the car and talk?" he asked.

With a trembling hand, she opened the door. She sat in the driver's seat and Ben got in the passenger seat. "Can we drive out of this parking lot?" he asked.

She said, "Am I safe? Can I trust you?"

He shrugged and said, "You are such a nice woman. You are very pretty and sincere. But I'm not trying to take advantage of your husband or you. We cannot stay here and talk. There are cameras in this parking lot."

He gave her instructions to drive, and asked her to pull over in an empty parking lot near a warehouse. "If you are worried I'll harm you, call your husband. Let our affairs be on a conference call. I don't mind. He may be panicking since you are not home by now. I want all of us to be on the phone—that will let you know that I'm a very sincere person."

Lucinda looked at him. Her eyes were cold. "Sincere? You've led my husband into sin. How sincere is sleeping with a married man?"

He scratched the nape of his neck and said, "Sincerity is in the eye of the beholder. Call your husband on the phone. Put him on the speaker and let us talk."

She did as he asked, and Dr. Mars answered the phone after a few rings. "Hi Honey," Lucinda said, trying to sound calm. "Ben is here with me in the car. I left the restaurant. He didn't show up, but he was by the car waiting for me in the rain."

"Are you sure you're safe?" Dr. Mars said, slurring his words. "You might be harmed!"

"No, that's why he requested that I call you, so that you'll know I'm safe," Lucinda said. "He said he is sincere."

Ben cut in. "Hey, Filip, how are you? You doing OK? I'm here in the car with your wife; she's sitting with me. Filip, all I want is money. I have video clips of you and me; I have our conversations on tape. I am not blackmailing you, but I need this money to take care of myself. I need a lot of care. I'm by myself—I'm practically homeless. I'm like a leech on you, I know, but I swear I'm not blackmailing you, I just need help, and you're the only one who can give it to me."

Dr. Mars shouted into the phone. "You're a prostitute. You're leeching on me. I'm the only one who can give you help because out of all your clients, I'm the only one who's rich enough. You're leeching on me, and I will drag you in the trenches."

Ben was quiet for a moment. "Filip, you don't understand me. I need money to take care of myself. I'm not a prostitute. You're not one of my richest clients. We satisfied needs in each other's lives. We both benefited from what we did. That doesn't make me a prostitute."

Lucinda spoke before they could continue to fight. "Let's talk. Ben, my husband and I can't afford a one million dollar blackmail fee."

"I said this isn't blackmail," Ben repeated.

"Call it what you like," Lucinda said. "My husband is well liked and well known in the community. If you leak these tapes, it will tear him apart. I do not support gays, and when I met my husband, I never knew what he was. But he has spoken with me; he has asked for forgiveness. He loves me from the bottom of his heart."

Lucinda smiled and continued. "The Devil got to my husband, and he went to you. So I need you to tell me the minimum amount of money we need to pay you to get those videotapes and to get you out of this town."

Ben thought. "You want me out of town?"

"Yes."

"And why?"

"Because you are evil."

Dr. Mars spoke from the phone. "Yes, I agree with you. We will pay you. Just leave town. If you don't, I will kill you with my bare hands."

Ben had been composed, but when Dr. Mars threatened him, he became livid. "Oh come on, you liar," he spat at the phone. "You can't kill me with your bare hands. You can't do fuck. Unlike your community, I have no respect for you. I'm not going to deal with you. I'm going to talk with your wife, a nice person." Ben flipped Lucinda's phone shut. Lucinda grimaced.

"How much is the least you'll accept?"

Ben asked, "Can you give me half a million?"

Without pausing, she said no. "My husband is not as rich as you think, Ben. Running a private practice is very expensive. However, I do have some money from a family inheritance, and I will give it to you. I'll give you 250 thousand dollars, and that's my only and final offer. Remember, we could take this up with the police, face the shame, and get you locked up behind bars."

"250 thousand?" Ben repeated.

"Yes. You will give me the videos you have and move out of the town. Period. If you don't, I will go to the police. I will bring my husband to the public to confess what he has done. After he confesses, I will hug him and kiss him in public. A lot of his patients will return to him, and I will comfort him. I will make him feel like a man again."

He kept quiet. For several minutes, the only sounds were the rain pelting the car and the distant thunder.

"Can I touch your forehead?" Ben asked.

Lucinda felt strong and willful. She told him no. "You are impure," she told him. "You want the money, so tell me where to bring it. Give me a week."

Ben pulled a paper from his pocket, and he drew up the route for her from her house to the cornfield. Lucinda looked at the route and thought, no wonder he comes back with so much mud on his tires.

"I'm not afraid of you," Lucinda told Ben before driving him back to the restaurant parking lot. "Worst-case scenario, if you do not give me everything I have demanded, I will personally confess to everybody in town. And they will forgive me, I guarantee you."

He shook her hand. "Done deal," he said. When she took him back to the restaurant, she watched him climb into the red truck. She shook her head and thought, this is where my husband has been making love.

Lucinda drove home slowly. She did not cry. She thought about what she had done wrong, and how she could have better satisfied her husband. When she got home, she went straight to talk to him. He was very drunk and looked so tired.

"We're not going to call the police," she told him. "Ben has agreed to 250 thousand. He told me how to get to the cornfield. In a week, I will take the money to him. This should never have happened, but now that it has, we are going to bury it."

Dr. Mars said, "So he wants 250 thousand?"

"Yes, I'll pay him for the evidence against you," Lucinda said. "I'm going to use my inheritance money."

"But is he going to leave town?" Dr. Mars asked anxiously.

"Yes, he promised."

"But Lucinda, you don't understand," Dr. Mars whined. "This guy is a leech. He set me up. I haven't been in a homosexual relationship for a long time. He smelled me out, he found me. He wanted to take advantage of me, and he did."

Lucinda stared at him, and for the first time, responded in anger. "Well you're stupid, Filip. You went for it. Now what can I do except give him what he wants?"

Dr. Mars began to cry again. "You'll give him the money and he'll give you the video clips, but he'll be back. I can't believe this mess. We're talking about a quarter of a million dollars, and he's going to come back. He's going to come hunting for us."

"I don't know, I don't think so," Lucinda says. "He might be the Devil, but he does seem sincere."

The following Sunday, Lucinda placed the money in a paper bag. She had collected it from six different accounts. She drove to the cornfield, and couldn't overcome the eerie sensation that she had been somewhere similar before.

Before she left, Lucinda called her husband, who had told her he was at the clinic. "I'm going to give him this money and get the tapes, and we're going to take it from there."

Bullshit, he thought. As he hung up with Lucinda, he pulled up to a small shack in the cornfield—the same shack where he had discovered Ben was living when he secretly followed him home from work a few days ago. Dr. Mars had his pistol with him.

Ben's shack was dilapidated and worn down. The window's shutters hung from its hinges, and the green paint was peeling off the roof and walls. Dr. Mars pulled his penknife from his pocket to cut a hole in the window screen, but saw that it was already hanging loose. He pulled it aside and climbed into the house.

Sweating and short of breath, Dr. Mars crept through the house. He realized quickly that Ben wasn't home. Maybe he would meet Lucinda after all, he thought.

He pulled his gun out of his pocket, pointed it at the ceiling, and shot one bullet. It was the first time he had ever shot the pistol, and it sounded much louder than he expected. He jumped, and fell to his knees on the ground, shaking. He stood back up, brushed off his knees, and began to walk through the house.

A fluorescent light shone in the living room. Flies swarmed around the gritty bulb. In the kitchen, the sink was full of dirty plates. Dr. Mars felt filthy just walking through the house, and he stepped into the bathroom to wash his hands.

As he turned on the faucet, Dr. Mars saw a box of medication on the corner of the counter. That bastard, he thought. Always begging for drugs for his fever, and he's already got some poor sap to prescribe him something else. He turned off the sink and dried his hands on his jeans. Then, he picked up the box.

"Shit." One word, spoken out loud, before he dropped the box on the sink. A bottle of pills fell out, and he lifted it to eye level. On it was Ben's name. Inside the bottle was a medication for HIV.

Dr. Mars sat down on the toilet seat and looked in the mirror at himself. He said, "Jesus, Lord. How can you punish me like this?" And he thought, I am so, so stupid. I can't believe I did this.

He imagined his wife waiting for Ben in the cornfield. He knew that Ben wasn't home, but he also knew he'd never show up there. With numb fingers, Dr. Mars dialed his wife's number on his phone.

"Did he come?"

"No, I'm still waiting for him," she said. "Where are you at?"

He hesitated. He couldn't feel his lips. "I'm in the office."

"But you're calling me from your cell phone."

"Yes," he responded.

"OK. Look, Filip, if he doesn't show up, I'll come home and we'll go to the police. We have to face this together. You'll have to confess."

"I love you," he said. He repeated it. "I love you so much. There's so much that you don't know."

Dr. Mars hung up the phone, got in his car, and drove to his office. As he was driving, he felt his body swell with pain. At first, he thought he must have been imagining it. But no—his limbs were hard and aching, his head was tense and throbbing, his eyes were too weak to see. He thought, there's no way to make this pain go away.

When he got to his office, he parked his car in the spot marked "Dr. Filip Mars" and went in. He sat down on the floor of his office, in front of his desk. He pulled out the vodka from his briefcase, remembering the gun was still in his pocket. He drank the vodka without tasting it, without feeling the burn. Everything was either numb or full of pain. They seemed to be almost the same sensation.

Dr. Mars thought about his wife, and the happy years they had together before he met Ben. He thought about his patients who refused to make positive changes in their lives. Finally, he thought about Ben.

He imagined Ben walking toward him. "What can we do now?" Ben asked.

He listened to himself talk. "You never told me you have HIV."

Ben grinned at him. "It's people in high places like you that judge me, that use me. This time, I used you. Dr. Filip Mars—the preacher, the saint. Now you are nothing but another person faced with a disease that he cannot handle."

Dr. Mars finished the vodka in the bottle. He thought he might be crying, but he couldn't feel the tears, and his large hands were too heavy to lift to his face. Good Lord, he thought, I have no more strength. I am like a wilted shrub, like the dead grass. What can I do now?

He felt the handle of the gun against the thigh in his pocket. And he thought for a very long time. Then, as he reached for the handle, Lucinda's kind face flashed before his eyes. "We will conquer," she said.

As Lucinda waited in the cornfield for Ben to arrive to collect his money, she couldn't quiet the heavy beating in her chest or the terrible thoughts in her mind. He wasn't going to come—he couldn't come. The things her husband and she would have to do would not be easy. They would not be happy. But she had confidence in the Good Lord that they would be right.

Then, she heard the distant sound of tires crunching on gravel. Was Ben going to show after all? Would they be able to put all of this behind them? She reached toward the brown paper bag sitting in the passenger seat, patting the sack full of money as the car came closer. She searched for the dot of red that would be Ben's truck coming over the horizon.

The dot was not red, she realized with a start. It was black, and it was rapidly getting closer.

It's Filip, she thought. But though she smiled, her entire body tensed. It's my husband, the preacher.

What does he have to preach about now?

978-0-595-47387-8
0-595-47387-3

1853911

Made in the USA